William-R. Brownlow

Memoir of Sir James Marshall

taken chiefly from his own letters

MEMOIR OF

SIR JAMES MARSHALL,

C.M.G.,

KNIGHT COMMANDER OF THE ORDER OF ST. GREGORY THE GREAT.

Taken chiefly from his own Letters.

BY

W. R. BROWNLOW

Canon of Plymouth.

BURNS AND OATES, LIMITED.

London :
28, Orchard Street, W.

New York :
Catholic Publication
Society Co.

1890.

SIR JAMES MARSHALL, C.M.G., K.C.S.G.

William-R. Brownlow

Memoir of Sir James Marshall

William-R. Brownlow

Memoir of Sir James Marshall
taken chiefly from his own letters

ISBN/EAN: 9783741157967

Manufactured in Europe, USA, Canada, Australia, Japa

Cover: Foto ©Raphael Reischuk / pixelio.de

Manufactured and distributed by brebook publishing software
(www.brebook.com)

CHAPTER VI.

**Requiem æternam dona ei, Domine,
Et Lux perpetua luceat ei!**

CHAPTER I.

EARLY LIFE.   CONVERSION.   EDGBASTON.
LETTERS FROM DR. NEWMAN.   THE BAR.

JAMES MARSHALL was born at Edinburgh, on
December 19, 1829. His father was at that time
Presbyterian minister of the Tolbooth Church,
which is the eastern portion of St. Giles' Cathedral. His mother was a daughter of the Rev.
Legh Richmond, whose *Annals of the Poor* were
so well known in Protestant families a generation
ago. In 1841, Mr. Marshall, senior, after long and
anxious deliberation, became convinced of the
Divine institution of Episcopacy, and at great
sacrifice of position, income, and ties of friendship,
resigned his office in the Scotch Presbyterian
Church, and eventually, in 1847, was appointed to
Christ Church, Clifton, of which church he was
minister until his death, in 1855. James was the
fifth of a family of twelve children, of whom six
died before their father. When he was sixteen, a
gun in the bow of a boat that he was pulling
ashore on Lundy Island accidentally went off, and
the whole charge passed through the upper part of
his right arm, which had to be taken off at the

B

shoulder. For several days he lay between life and death, but at length his strength returned, and he soon learned to write with his left hand, and became so dexterous, that people who met him in society hardly noticed the loss he had sustained. Before this accident took place, James had an ardent wish to enter the army, and serve in India, and his father had gone so far as to apply for a cadetship. The army was now out of the question, and in 1847 he entered Exeter College, Oxford, and after taking his degree, became an Anglican minister in 1852, and his first curacy was at a small village called Trysull, not far from Wolverhampton. In 1854, he became curate to the late Rev. W. Denton, of St. Bartholomew's, Moor Lane, in the parish of St. Giles', Cripplegate.

Whatever James Marshall took in hand, he did it with all his might. When he made up his mind to be an Anglican clergyman, he determined to devote himself heart and soul to his work. The same principles that had led his father to embrace Episcopacy led most of his children to go far beyond himself in a High Church direction.[1] Before he went to London, James had fallen under the influence of a movement which had for its main object the infusion into the sacramental and sacerdotal system of Puseyism the personal piety and inward conversion to God insisted upon by the early Evangelicals. It is difficult to form an accurate judgment of religious movements among

[1] Mr. Marshall, senior, had, in a paper read before "The Kirk Session," said, "The main question is, Has the great Head of the Church left us any intimation of His will respecting the way in which His Church was to be governed?" (*Life*, p. 79.)

the various bodies that have separated from the Church. The Church has pronounced clearly upon the heresies which caused their separation, but she does not concern herself with their subsequent developments. Catholics therefore form widely divergent opinions as to the relative proportion of good or evil in such movements. The effect of this influence on the mind of Mr. Marshall was to deepen in him those habits of prayer which he had learned in childhood, to set his heart on fire with a personal love of our Lord Jesus Christ, and to make him ready for any sacrifice for the glory of God and the salvation of souls. He threw himself with all his soul into his work among the coster-mongers, and the crowds of poor people, who thronged the courts and alleys near Moor Lane. He and his fellow-curates preached out of doors and in rooms in these courts, while at the same time he took the greatest pains in improving the music and other external parts of public worship in the church. His bright and joyous temperament, his warm, affectionate heart, his tender sympathy with affliction of every kind, and his firm and delicate treatment of difficult cases that came under his notice, caused him to be much appreciated and beloved; and many who did not have the happiness to follow him into the Catholic Church, still retain a deep sense of love and respect for him.

It is necessary to bear these things in mind in order to understand what an immense sacrifice it was to him to give up so much that seemed good work, and become a nonentity in the Catholic Church. The loss of his arm, which had not been considered a bar to his becoming an Anglican preacher, was an insuperable obstacle in the way of his becoming a Catholic priest. As happens so often with earnest-minded Anglicans, he had to listen to and attempt to satisfy the difficulties of several young men in the congregation. Some other young London clergymen were in the same difficulties. The mutual discussion of their misgivings deepened instead of dissipating them. "We were at it till past midnight," he wrote, "and all I could see at the end was, that if the Pope is not the Vicar of Jesus Christ, he must be Antichrist, and that I must be either a Roman or a Protestant. . . . All seem going on as I have done, dreading lest there might be a mine under their feet, but not liking to dig and see." Unable any longer to bear the suspense, Marshall and a clerical friend, who has been for the last thirty years a devoted Catholic priest, sought an interview with Father Edmund Vaughan, at the Redemptorist Monastery, Clapham. Marshall's main point was the Papal Supremacy, his friend's great difficulty was the Catholic devotion to our Lady. To the amusement of Father Vaughan, Marshall, who had long had a tender devotion to the Blessed Virgin, refuted all his friend's objections on that score, while his friend supplied the solution to most of his difficulties about the Pope. Father Vaughan said, "Well, you two will very soon convert one another." A short time afterwards he resigned his curacy, and wrote from his mother's house :

I have gone through as much, almost more than mind and body can sustain, and the fierceness of the conflict is now over, and I am already entering on the actual *posses-*

sion of that glorious inheritance of the children of God, which I have already deeply enjoyed in the *hope* that I had it. God has enabled me to exercise an abstract faith in His Church, though it was always attended by an aching doubt that perhaps it was exercised in a wrong position and object. It has proved so, but all doubt is now passing away, and certainty taking its place. . . . I shall knock boldly at the gate, and that gate will be opened to me, and I shall be safe with Jesus and Mary, Saints and Angels, in the Bosom of God. It is very hard to flesh and blood, but the worst is, I hope, passed ; but if not, so be it.

This letter was written November 11, 1857, and he was received into the Church on the 21st of November, by the late Father Coffin, who died Bishop of Southwark, and with whom James Marshall remained to the last on terms of most affectionate friendship. From that day, not a shadow of doubt seems to have ever darkened his mind, and he could say : *Elegi abjectus esse in domo Dei mei, magis quam habitare in tabernaculis peccatorum.*

The position of an Anglican clergyman who becomes a Catholic is always surrounded with more or less difficulty. His whole mind has generally been wrapped up in ecclesiastical matters, he has been looked up to as a teacher and guide, with a number of persons and various charitable organizations depending upon him. He finds himself suddenly regarded as a neophyte, whose duty is to learn and not to teach, and whose opinion on matters spiritual, theological, or ecclesiastical, is not only of no weight, but suspected to have an heretical tinge. If he finds a vocation to the priesthood, his course is clear and simple. But if

that course is closed to him, and he has not means
of his own, he finds himself reduced to a painful
struggle for existence, and is obliged to seek for a
livelihood in occupations always strange to him,
and often uncongenial. Cardinal (then Dr.) Manning
kindly offered Mr. Marshall the office of Procurator,
and Precentor, and for some two or three years he
found a home with the Oblates of St. Charles at
Bayswater.   His musical knowledge enabled him
to direct the choir, and his love for children made
him very useful in the school, which has since
grown into St. Charles' College.   But the living in
daily intercourse with the priests, and the constant
attendance at the altar, where he could never offer
the Holy Sacrifice, kept his position too painfully
before him.   Some time after he had left, he wrote
thus :

When I found my life at Bayswater did but crush me
more and more under the bitter trial of being excluded
from ministering at the altar ; and that I could not enter
the cloister either, I had to enter upon the position of a
Christian gentleman in the world. I did so, and very
queer it was for a time : but my aim was to establish
myself distinctly in that character.

He took a situation as tutor in a Catholic family,
but eventually found a much more congenial
occupation as one of the masters in the Oratory
School at Edgbaston, " where," he writes in 1863,
" I still am, and believe myself to be one of the
happiest creatures on the earth." He gives an
account of the daily life in the school, and says :

The general tone of the school is most admirable,
and a cause of the most deep gratitude to all engaged
in it. . . . Another immense blessing is the real fraternal

love that exists among the masters, as well as the open-hearted affectionate standing we are upon with the boys. We are quite dependent on each other for society, as unfortunately we have no other here ; so it is fortunate we pull so well together.

The writer of this memoir may be pardoned a slight digression here, since his friend's position at the Oratory was in a great measure instrumental in his own conversion to the faith. He asked Mr. Marshall to obtain for him a reply to some difficulties he had on the subject of the " Priest's Intention " in administering the sacraments, and especially in the consecration of the Holy Eucharist. The two following letters from Cardinal (then Dr.) Newman will show the patience of the late Cardinal in dealing with somewhat unreasonable difficulties.

LETTER I.

July 9th, 1863.

My dear Mr. Marshall,—In answer to your friend's question, I will say, " The Roman Church *does* teach that it rests entirely with the priest to make a valid sacrament."

This is plain from the *form* of words, not to say the *matter*, being simply in his power. Even in the rite itself, he might put no wine into the chalice, or so much water compared with the wine that it was not matter for consecration. And again, he might purposely leave out some words of the form. It is certain, then, *quite independently* of the doctrine of what is technically called "intention," and of all questions of the *sort* of intention necessary, he has power over the consecration, in having power over the matter and form. And, I suppose, if "he maliciously intended to make the sacrament a sham," he would do so, *not* by withholding his *intention* to consecrate, but by effecting that non-intention by an actual invalidating of *form* and *matter*.

Speaking then by-the-bye, I will say that is some

wonder to me that Protestant controversialists should
lay such stress upon our doctrine of intention, con-
sidering, even in the Anglican rite, the celebrant has
power over the form and matter, and could, if he were
wicked, mutilate either.

This is, however, by-the-bye; for I grant that with us
the question has this additional importance, that, not
only is the Blessed Sacrament food to the communicant,
but an *object of worship* to the faithful generally.

I cannot then say anything in opposition to your
friend's words, " I do not see how you can ever be *sure
infallibly* of the intention of the priest who consecrated
the Blessed Sacrament."

He infers from this, " I do not see how you can ever
be sure that you do not *commit idolatry* in adoring the
Blessed Sacrament."

On this I make two remarks:

1. That I must *enlarge* the difficulty exceedingly, if it
is one. For generally the Blessed Sacrament is adored,
not simply as exposed, but when concealed in the tabernacle. Now nothing is more common than for stupid or
heedless people, for children, nay for ourselves, who are
neither stupid, nor heedless, nor children, to make a
mistake as to the particular tabernacle in which the
Blessed Sacrament is reserved. In our own church, we
have, as you know, tabernacles at two, not to say three
altars; and for the sake of reverence (as when the altar
is being cleaned), the Blessed Sacrament is sometimes
moved from one to another altar. One perhaps takes for
granted that It is in Its ordinary place, and it is quite
possible to be in this error during the ordinary time of a
visit; nay, it is most difficult not to forget the removal,
even after knowing it, and to relapse, while on one's
knees into the mistake. Now everything ought to be
done, and is done, to prevent all this, but it cannot
altogether be prevented.

If then there is any serious fault in adoring wrongly,
it is certainly not a rare fault. Yet in parallel cases, we
do not think much of such a mistake. If you spoke to
one man as if he were another, if you treated a great
man rudely, taking him for a little man, if I took a

youth I met at Windsor or at Oxford for the Prince of Wales, and paid him honours which none but the Prince could claim, I do not suppose that in either case, whether the great man was neglected, or the little· man made much of instead of him, that the great man would be offended, if he had common sense; nor should *I* be annoyed, *except* as thinking that, since he *could not* know the state of the case, *he* might be surprised and annoyed. And therefore in the religious matter an Omniscient God, and a God who has made religion for man as man, for a weak, ignorant, fallible frail creature, and for the mass of men, not the clear-sighted only, the collected and the prudent, and who knows therefore that infinite mistakes *must* occur, and that sacred things, if they were vouchsafed, must, in a way, be given to dogs. He surely will not impute it heavily to any one that he mistakes the place of the Divine Presence, provided that there is no great and gross carelessness.

If it be not so, then, we need not go to the question of the priest's intention, to be sure that there are innumerable acts of idolatry committed ordinarily in the Catholic Church.

2. This leads me, secondly, to say that Catholic divines recognize the remarks, which I have been drawing out, by applying here the distinction, which is serviceable in so many other cases, between *formal* and *material* acts.

For instance. The Greek Church is schismatical, its people are schismatics, but A, B, and C are not in *formal* schism, but in *material* schism, *i.e.*, they are *in loco schismaticorum*, but they need not be more, they need not have that internal mould, character, purpose, &c., which constitutes sin and guilt.

And in like manner, though we should say that the Anglican Church was in heresy, we should not say that individual members of it were *formal* heretics.

And in like manner, the act of the Catholic who mistakes an unconsecrated host for a consecrated (an act, observe, so very, very rare, that I never heard of even the suspicion of one instance of it), commits an act of *material* idolatry at most, that is, he makes a mistake.

I have not answered the main question about the Council of Trent, Bellarmine, &c., upon the doctrine of intention, because I thought it beside the mark, but I will do so, if Mr. B——— wishes.

Yours very truly,
JOHN H. NEWMAN.

LETTER II.

July 11th, 1863.

MY DEAR MR. MARSHALL,—Your friend's words which misled me were those in which he summed up the difficulty as to our doctrine which he wished cleared up. He spoke as if it was specially the *practical* difficulty.

1. He said: "If (the doctrine) means what Protestants take it to mean," (that, I suppose, that the priest's intention is in such sense internal that he may withhold it), " I do not see how you can ever be sure that *you do not commit idolatry* in adoring the Blessed Sacrament; because you cannot be *infallibly sure of the intention* of the priest who consecrated It."

I said in answer to this,

(1) That I *granted* that I " did not see how we could ever be infallibly sure of the intention of the priest who consecrated the Blessed Sacrament."

(2) That I *denied* that we could be committing idolatry, even though the priest *had* withheld his intention. And this I went on to show.

2. Your friend said, too, as explaining himself: "What I want to know is, Does the Roman Church teach that it rests entirely with the priest to make a valid sacrament or not?"

To this I answered with equal distinctness:

"The Roman Church *does* teach that it rests entirely with the priest to make a valid sacrament." And this is plain, whatever becomes of the doctrine of intention, from the fact that it is the priest who takes the matter into his hands and utters the form.

3. These two questions he put as *explanations* of the purely doctrinal question, with which he began, about

the interpretation of a Canon of the Council of Trent, and which I said I was willing to answer if he wished it, but which I did not answer because there is so little that can be said about it.

The question is this as he stated it:

"What does the Roman Church understand *to be the meaning of* the decree of the Council of Trent, Sess. VII. can. xi. *De Sacramentis?*"

By "the meaning" I suppose your friend to be asking whether the intention spoken of in that Canon is external or internal?

My only answer is, "I do not know, nor does any one know." The Church has never explained herself; and divines have variously interpreted her. It is not a *practical question*, as I have said already, while the form and matter are still left to the priest; and I have never felt interest in it.

The most prevalent opinion just now, as far as I know, is, that the *internal* intention of the priest is necessary. So Father Perrone maintains, grounding his views chiefly upon the condemnation passed by Alexander VIII. on the following proposition, and which Benedict XIV. says is a *grave vulnus* to the doctrine of the external intention:

"Valet Baptismus collatus a ministro, qui omnem ritum externum formamque baptizandi observet, intus vero in corde suo apud se resolvit: Non intendo facere quod facit Ecclesia." And on the Rubrics of the Missal approved by Clement VIII., in which the consecration made by a priest "qui habens coram se undecim hostias, intendit consecrare solum decem, non determinans quas decem intendet," is declared to be *irrita*.

But I have heard divines say that the Church still leaves the question of the external or internal intention open, in spite of these authorities later than Trent. And I am told this view is growing.

I have not a word more or less than this to say, in answer to your friend's question. I know nothing more; nor do I think any more is known; that is, as to the abstract point. There is no difficulty in practice.

Yours very truly,

JOHN H. NEWMAN.

Mr. Marshall's correspondent was led, by the
frankness of these letters, to write directly to
Dr. Newman on other points, and Mr. Marshall
had the consolation of singing *Te Deum* at his
friend's reception into the Church in the following
November.

His friendly relations with the masters and for
the Fathers at Edgbaston continued unbroken
to the end of his life. Cardinal Newman and
all the Fathers had an affectionate regard for him,
he was always a welcome guest at the Oratory.
He was always extremely popular with the boys.
His skill at racquets and football, in spite of the
loss of his arm, his frank and genial disposition,
and his love of fun endeared him to them. When
he left they presented him with a testimonial,
saying they had ever found him "a kind friend
and a considerate master." The late Serjeant
Bellasis, whose sons had all been Mr. Marshall's
pupils at the Oratory, frequently visited Father
Newman, and it was chiefly by his advice that
James Marshall availed himself of the law which
now enables ex-parsons to divest themselves of
their clerical disabilities, and he entered himself
at Lincoln's Inn, and in due course was called
to the bar.

In 1866, he attached himself to the Northern
Circuit, and took up his abode at Manchester.
He was considered fortunate to make over £80 in
his first year, and he had several pupils, chiefly
young Frenchmen and Germans, who wished to
study English Law. In his Anglican days,
Mr. Marshall had assisted at the starting of the
Union newspaper ; and thus, in conjunction with

Dr. F. G. Lee, Lord Beauchamp, and others, may be said to have originated the Ritualistic movement. At Manchester, he had much to do with the foundation of the *Catholic Times*, as afterwards in the short-lived publication of the *Catholic Press.* In politics he was a Liberal, and an ardent Home Ruler, but he never allowed his party predilections to influence him when any Catholic interest was at stake. The Franco-Prussian War swept away all his pupils, and he was glad to accept the offer made to him in 1873 of the appointment of Chief Magistrate and Judicial Assessor to the native tribes on the Gold Coast, at a town called Cape Coast.

CHAPTER II.

THE position and work of the Chief Magistrate on the Gold Coast will be best understood by some extracts from his own *Reminiscences :*

I used to preside in a court along with the chiefs, and we heard native cases involving native laws and customs, principally in connection with land. This gave me a good insight into the real state of the people, apart from the changes and innovations brought by Europeans. The chiefs, through an interpreter, expounded the native laws, which had been handed down from time immemorial, through the perpetual succession of chiefs and headmen. . . . As Judicial Assessor to the chiefs, I found myself in the position of a head chief, and I do not think any better office could have been created, as it was so well calculated to reconcile the chiefs and people to the changes brought by Europeans, and to adjust the differences which of necessity arose. The Judicial Assessor's duty was to use all that was good and useful in the native laws and customs, and as far as possible to preserve these for the natives, and at the same time to introduce Christian justice among them. . . . I liked my duties very much, and used to take the greatest interest in sitting with the chiefs, listening to them. . . . They came to the court, dressed in handsome native cloths, made mostly of thick silk, which sat upon them in graceful folds, like the drapery of the ancient Roman in his *toga.* They wore quantities of gold ornaments on their arms and fingers, and were attended by their captains, sword-bearers, and numerous followers, who sat in a picturesque group round their respective chiefs, each of whom sat upon his "stool." The refined and simple eloquence of these chiefs, or their "linguists" in speaking for them, both in their gestures and their language, impressed me greatly. I also soon found that the chiefs, as well as the people, when the white man in authority treated them with courtesy and fairness, would look upon him as a friend, and both serve and obey when it was due. Unfortunately, the Englishman generally looks upon the "nigger" as a creature to be sworn at and kicked, and laughs at his ridiculous kings and customs.

The Ashanti War brought out the truth of this, vividly. Those officers who treated the natives kindly, and were patient and persevering with them, were in the end able to lead them anywhere, and could depend upon them in the greatest emergencies. A brave band of scouts headed the expedition, and were in front all the way to Coomassi. They were led by a gallant young officer, Lord Gifford, to whom they were deeply attached, as he became to them. Many of them fell fighting bravely, and it was with them that Lord Gifford won the Victoria Cross.

Even my peaceful duties as a Judge gave me so much personal influence over the chiefs of the Cape Coast and their people, that I was found to be the only white man they would follow, and at their request I was for a time in the field at the head of a large contingent.[1]

It must be remembered that he had not been five months in the country, when this testimony to his firm, just, and conciliatory conduct was given. His empty right sleeve gave the natives additional confidence in his generalship, as they regarded him as a veteran who had lost his arm in battle. Some extracts from his letters to his

[1] *Reminiscences*, pp. 11—15.

mother and sisters during the war will be read
with interest. The little personal details were
naturally intended only for the family circle :

Cape Coast, Oct. 28th, 1873.—Yesterday, I went out
to the camp, walking both ways. I went with an escort
taking charge of some powder and a gun, and armed
with a loaded revolver, in case we should be attacked.
When we arrived, all the natives were being drilled, and
the chiefs and captains were delighted to see me. My
chief object was to get them rifles, and after all these
months of war, they have not yet got them. But I got
one hundred and twenty for them, and as carriers are
now scarce, women carried them out. Hundreds of
women are now busily employed in transport, and do it
a deal better than the men, working harder, and very
merrily. As each batch arrived last evening at the
camp, I harangued them through an interpreter to drive
out the men left behind, at which they shouted with
glee. . . . There was a little moonlight, and I thoroughly
enjoyed my walk : the strange march through the bush,
with crowds of fire-flies brightening the path, and amidst
the noise and cries of all kinds of insects, birds, and
animals. I carried my revolver in my hand, but again
brought it back loaded.

Nov. 4th.—I have been for some days without any
letter on the stocks for anybody, for the reason that,
much to my own astonishment and yours too, if you
could only have seen me, I have been taking an active
part in the campaign, even to leading out a party in
search of the enemy. On Friday morning last I started
very early for Fort Napoleon, to see my chiefs and
Cape Coast people. We had a lovely walk in the cool
morning, and I found the truth of what Mr. Maurice
had told me, that that is the only time to see the wild
flowers in all their beauty. There were numbers of the
most lovely Passion-flowers I ever saw. Convolvuluses of
every size and colour, and numberless other flowers, in
the midst of the general tangle of vegetation that prevails
everywhere here. I arrived at Fort Napoleon as fresh
as a daisy, and over a camp-breakfast in a hut of palm-

leaves, I heard a dreadfully bad account of the Cape Coast chiefs and men. The captain in charge of the fort had quite given them up, and it seems they positively refused to move on to Dunquah, the place of general meeting. Presently I had them all before me, read them a proclamation from the Governor [Sir Garnet Wolseley], and told them, if they hesitated, he would have no more to do with them, nor would I. I waxed so eloquent, as I heard the interpreter throwing it into them, that at last I said: "If you will start at once, I will go at your head." Without a moment's delay, the answer was: "We are ready, we will go with your honour at once." This took me aback; so I had to explain, that I must send in to the Governor. I did so, and spent an easy sort of day in the camp. No answer came till sunset; and then I received Sir Garnet's sincere thanks,[1] with a request to lead my forces as soon as possible to a place called Beulah, accompanied by a Marine Artillery officer, Lieutenant Allen, and then at once to get in contact with the enemy, and harass them! This was a big go! I meant to march with them, and see them on the way, and then return to Cape Coast, but of course I accepted the position.

I had made no preparations for camping out; but a blanket, waterproof sheet, and revolver were sent out to me, and I sent in for a few things, food and wine. In the moonlight, I went down to the camp, and assembled

---

[1] The following was Sir Garnet's letter:

My dear Judge,—Your movement this morning has been most satisfactory. I am very much obliged to you for the trouble you have taken. I intend pushing on the force now at Napoleon to Beulah on Monday. I send Colonel Wood to Beulah to-morrow, to take command there, so I do not think it will be necessary for you to postpone your Session on Monday. I dare say that before long I shall ask you to use your influence with the C.C. people again, for your endeavours have been very successful. Perhaps you had better return here to-morrow evening, so as to be able to begin your judicial work on Monday. Again thanking you very sincerely, believe me always very truly yours,

G. J. WOLSELEY.

Captain Huyshe, who will give you this, will convey to you what I wish done. I am sending you out four hundred rifles and accoutrements.

C

the chiefs; and then I found myself sitting by their camp-fires and the pale ghostly light of the moon, exhorting them to go bravely with me in the morning. I slept with an officer in a palm-hut, within the fort, lying on palm-leaves; but the mosquitoes were too awful to allow of sleep. I made my puggery a kind of net, but had to leave a breathing-hole, and soon I found my poor nose swelling up horridly. I was not sorry to get up, and after some trouble and exhortation, got my regiment of one thousand niggers under weigh, with drums, horns, and flags. My companion, Lieutenant Allen, was a very pleasant one, and we kept each other up during an awfully hot march, happily only of an hour and a half. At one place we came across a river, with great boulders and trees so like North Wales, and here there was a general halt, and scouts sent on to see if Beulah was clear of the enemy. Hearing it was all right, we headed our forces with Chief Attah and a few in front, and we soon came to the place, which proved most lovely. We had passed through wonderful vegetation, and here were trees beautiful beyond description. It was a flourishing Wesleyan station, and we found the bare walls of their house, which must have been a most pleasant one. We were in an awful state of heat and thirst, so you can imagine our delight at seeing lots of orange and lime trees, and what is still more delicious, green cocoa-nuts full of milk.

Nov. 9th.—The natives soon cleared a lot of bush, cutting down shrubs and trees that were sad to see, only they are mere weeds here; and as there were plenty of bamboo trees, they soon made huts in all directions, and built one in the centre for myself and Lieutenant Allen. It was a thorough picnic without the ladies, and without almost any of the necessary appliances of civilized life. Luckily, I had a supply of tins with me, and some wine; for the Control sent us nothing, and I had to feed Allen and a serjeant who accompanied me everywhere. After a good rest, I exhorted my chiefs and captains that the whole force was to turn out in the morning in search of the enemy, who were said to be immediately in front. But in the evening a Captain

Huyshe came out from Sir Garnet, and said that Beulah would be made an important camp, as the main body of the enemy, with their Commander-in-Chief, were all in the immediate neighbourhood preparing to attack another of our camps, Abrakrampa, and therefore we were not to make any attack, or expose any Europeans, but only to send out reconnoitring parties. I was not sorry for this, as these Fantis are not to be depended on for a moment, and I believe six Ashantis would make a hundred of them run. This was at sunset, and then we found that we had forgotten candles or lanterns. But there was moonlight and the camp-fires, and we were soon glad to lie down for the night. I was up early, and having declared to the chiefs that they must turn out against the enemy, I did not like to let it fall through, so ordered a party of three hundred to get ready to. go out with me, while the others cleared the bush. The work of getting these niggers to turn out of a morning is something dreadful. They must have their breakfast; and I fancy they don't like moving until the sun is well up, which is just what the white man avoids when he can. By great exertion I got my party ready, and started about seven with a company of thirty scouts in front who knew the country. For half an hour we had very heavy walking over broken hilly country in a bad broken path through thick bush. We then came to the Sweet River and lovely primæval forest, where the walking was delicious, and soon became extremely lively by the eager look-out of the scouts to see if any enemy was at hand. Presently we came to where the road or track divided; and the captain of the scouts told me we were near were his party had fired on some Ashantis two days before. I thought I had gone far enough, and asked them to go on, and examine further. The reply was to the effect that they could not very well, but would be highly pleased to do so with me. So on I went. But they put me well into the middle, and we continued our march in a long single file; not a word spoken above a whisper, and everybody in an attitude of preparation for a sudden attack from the bush on either side. We came upon numerous tracks of the enemy, recent fires, and

places where they had laid down; and then we came near
a village called Soroffoo, where they had been reported
as encamped two days before. I did not care about
risking an attack, but would not stand in the way of its
being done, so on we went.

Presently the captain whispered to me that he saw the
smoke of their camp-fires. I looked, and thought not;
but he sent on scouts to examine. They reported, No
one there, so on we went very gingerly; and soon we
came to the village, which they entered, throwing themselves out in different directions, lest the enemy should
be in ambush. I walked in, and confess I felt my
courage tested to a considerable stretch, as it seemed
very possible we might have a volley into us at any
moment, for there was a big camp. The village, like all
the others, is utterly destroyed by these brutes, and the
poor inhabitants scattered, enslaved, or murdered. But
there were numbers of huts erected, and cooking-pots
lying about, and some recent corpses that looked like a
hurried departure. Our men took some of these, and
back we went. On the way back, the scout company
persuaded me to go through a terribly thick path to
another destroyed village, where they had cut the head
off—and there I saw the headless body—of a huge
Ashanti. When we got back I lay down very hot and
tired, and what I now look upon as a very pretty girl
came and bathed my face and hand and feet, which was
very refreshing. I kept very quiet the rest of that day,
which turned out to be Sunday, but which until Captain
Huyshe's arrival I thought to be Saturday. Shortly
before sunset, my successor, Colonel Wood, arrived from
Elmina, with a most imposing array of more disciplined
troops than mine, with rockets, a gun, and above all a
horse, which made a tremendous sensation. I got away
as soon as I could, and after walking some distance was
not a little thankful to meet a hammock sent out for me.
It was my first ride in one, and it brought me in very
comfortably. I was a dirty untidy figure, as I had not
been able even to have a wash that day; but I went and
reported myself to the General, who was in Government
House with his Staff, sitting after dinner, and I was

received with great acclamations, and a big drink of claret and soda-water that was delicious.

Next day I was Judge again, it being my monthly Session, but there was little doing. In the evening I dined with Sir Garnet, and in the middle of dinner he received a despatch which I saw was bad news. It proved to be very bad news. An attack had been made upon the enemy from Dunquah, and one of the expedition, a fine young fellow, Eardley Wilmot, was shot dead through the heart. On Tuesday I again held court, and when sitting received word that I was again wanted at Beulah. The chiefs and captains had begged that I might be with them. My business was finished, and as Sir Garnet wished it, I at once acquiesced, especially as I thoroughly enjoyed · it.

In the morning I got a hammock, and off I went, with my boy Koffi and two bearers carrying food, &c. On arriving, my people testified great pleasure, and Colonel Wood at once asked me to get them all under weigh to move on. After the usual amount of palaver, threats, and entreaties, I got the companies out, and marched at their head to the end of the encampment, with their drums beating and their war-songs sounding through the place. At the edge of the bush I stopped to see them file by, but here the leading company refused to go on, under the excuse of not knowing the way. It was pure cowardice : and I had to get in an awful rage, and keep my serjeant interpreter calling them all sorts of names, until at last a few fellows, with I hope some pluck, led the way, and off they went, and I had a most pleasant quiet evening after they left. We had a scratch dinner, four of us, on a box, and I supplied some champagne, and we were quite a merry party. My people had built me another hut, and I slept profoundly. In the morning, I was awoke by an officer saying that Colonel Wood wished to see me. I scrambled out of the pajamas, which you happily sent me, into some clothes. The camp of Abrakrampa had been attacked by the enemy, and he was to move on, and attack them on the flank or rear. He asked me to go off at once, and catch up my people, and get them in that direction.

I got together my things as quickly as I could, and
started with my serjeant and Lieutenant Allen. The King
of Aguafoo had been ordered to provide me with an
escort of thirty men; and when I went for them, it was
the old story, they hadn't had their breakfast. No one was
ready. I abused and threatened His Majesty, and after
exertion and walking about that takes off most of one's
freshness, I got five or six and started off, the rest
coming after. It was the same route as before, only we
passed through Soroffoo to the next village. The stink
of dead bodies was horrid. Here I found my forces, and
told them what was wanted. The cowardly creatures
deceived me as to the road, advising that they should
go to a place called Assayboo. I asked if it led to
Abrakrampa, and, as they said Yes, I ordered them to
march instantly. Off they went, and we cooked a breakfast, and then Colonel Wood arrived with his forces;
and to my intense annoyance I found my Cape Coast
men had gone *away* from the enemy to a place on the
main road, where we had troops, in fact the first station
from Cape Coast. I was awfully annoyed, and thought
it useless to expend more strength on them. Colonel
Wood held a council with his officers, and decided he
would not venture on going on to attack with the force
at his command, but would also go to Assayboo, and
round that way to Abrakrampa itself. I was inclined
to turn back to Beulah, but thought I might meet some
Ashantis, so I marched also. To describe that march is
beyond mortal pen. The blazing sun scorched us
through and through, and I seemed really red-hot. It
was heavy bush walking, and though the trees and
vegetation and scenery were beautiful, it was far longer
than any of us supposed. On and on we went, till we
came to a steep hill, at the top of which were some
magnificent trees. Here Colonel Wood ordered a halt,
and I lay down almost speechless. My hope was that
he would encamp there; but not a bit of it, and again
we went on till another halt was called, and the doctor
told me I must get into a hammock. I was not sorry
to do so, and fell into the rear with the baggage. After
being carried some little way, I was nearly asleep, when

my bearers put me down, and I was told that our main body had been attacked. I listened, and there, for a certainty, was heavy firing going on. I got on my legs, and led the way at a great pace to catch up the others. But, after pressing on for some time, found there were no signs of them, and that I was almost by myself; so I waited for the baggage party to come up, and trusted my fate to theirs.

The sun set, and the heavy clouds made it very dark. The path became too rugged for a hammock, so on I walked till we came to an *inhabited* village—a strange sight. Here we found our main body had *not* been; but we got a guide to take us along. I thought I must stay there, but made one more attempt at being carried. I soon felt it was impossible, the men stumbled so, and out I got, and stumbled at almost every step, the path was so bad. Presently it went through dense thick bush, where it was often pitch dark, and I could only tell the way by feeling for the man in front of me. It was like a nightmare, made worse by occasional flashes of green lightning. At last we came to another village, and lay down for a few minutes, and then found ourselves in the main road which was being made up the country. Here I had to make them carry me again, and I fell asleep directly, and was awakened by a voice saying, "Is this an invalid officer?" "Yes," says some native. "Oh, dear, no," said I, tumbling out, and I found myself in an encampment held by blue-jackets and their officers. The delight of getting to Assayboo at last made me feel quite lively again, but it was nine o'clock, and I had started at 7.30 a.m. It was far too much for everybody. To our amazement we found that the main body had not arrived; but I at once agreed with the officer in charge, that we could do no more, and, whatever had become of them, we must stop there. So I accepted the offer of a corner of a room, in a house where several naval officers already lay, and then set my boy to cook some supper. Presently the main body arrived. Their guide had led them wrong, so we received them. I had no palm leaves that night to lie on, and thought of my spring mattress, but slept very well. My regiment, I found, had been sent on.

Next morning we were reinforced by some sailors and marines, and marched very leisurely to Abrakrampa. The first part was along the main road, quite a new one, made by the Engineers, and was beautiful ; the trees grand, with wonderful parasites, and undergrowth of bananas, and many others that I did not know. We then turned off into a bush-path towards Abrakrampa, where we found Sir Garnet and his Staff, and a large array of troops of every kind. The Ashantis had been attacking the place for two days with their main forces, and had kept it up nearly through one night, but without doing any harm, though they almost wore out the garrison, until Sir Garnet and his force arrived. I now found that my men had gained nothing by coming, and were told they were to advance against the enemy into the bush that afternoon. The bush had been cleared for about two hundred yards. I collected the chiefs, and told them ; and, at about 2.30 p.m., the whole place, from the General downwards, turned out to see them go. They spread out in long lines, and went across the space without a shot. They then paused, and evidently did not like to go further. This was too much for me ; and if I had only had my revolver, I think I must have led them in. But I only had my umbrella, so I followed them up and urged them to move in. Maurice followed me, and we used our umbrellas—in fact, he broke his— and at last they crowded in. Had a shot been fired, I fear there would have been a rush ; though I warned them they would be shot at and cut down if they ran away. But not a single shot came ; so we supposed that the enemy must be gone. Some of us then followed into the bush to see what was there, and found two bodies, and clots of blood in many places, but no great destruction. We then went back to the village, and in about an hour I heard that my people were engaged. I hastened to the part nearest, and there to be sure I heard the *bang bang* of rifles sounding merrily in the woods, with shouts and war-songs. Presently I was intensely gratified by seeing some women brought in, who had been carried off by these brutes. The first had her throat wounded with the incision of a knife, which her master had made, intending to cut her throat, when happily he was shot dead.[1] Then came other prisoners and spoil, and word that the Ashantis were in flight, and their camp taken.

The Houssas were then sent in, and away they went under my great friend Gordon. Had I seen him go, I should have followed him, as it was only a peremptory feeling of duty that restrained me. But as it turned out, there was no danger. The Ashantis were fairly broken, and in full flight, leaving guns, baggage, and everything behind; and so my cowardly regiment of frightened Fantis stumbled into a brilliant victory. This was evidently intensely annoying to those who had been hemmed up in the town for two days, hotly attacked; and more abuse than ever was lavished upon my people, and it was said that it wasn't even they who had done the firing, but another tribe. I know them to be such monstrous cowards, that I can't say much; but still I think they did this, and I am awfully sorry I didn't go in with them now. But I knew they might all run away, or fire so promiscuously, that they would be much more dangerous than the enemy.

Lots of spoil was brought in, including the drum, chair, and bedstead of the chief commander, who, the escaped prisoners said, was very drunk, which perhaps accounted for the surprise. The row on the return was immense. I spent a horrid night, slept uneasily, and

[1] Colonel Brackenbury gives some more details: "A young woman carrying her child on her back, was brought into Abrakrampa as a prisoner. On her neck was a slight cut, broad, and quite freshly made, from which blood was trickling. . . . She was a Commendah woman who had been captured some months before by the Ashantis, and had been kept as a slave by one of the chiefs. This man had grown fond of her; and when the first shots of our approaching skirmishers were heard, a few minutes before, he had ordered her to seize her child and some household goods, and to rush away with him. Before she had time to obey him, shots came nearer, and because she was slow, so she said, in his fear that he would not be able to carry her away, he had taken his knife and actually commenced to cut her throat, when he was shot down by one of our people. The mark on her throat, and the terrible frightened look in the eyes that had so recently looked death close in the face, were the best witnesses to the truth of her tale" (*Ashanti War*, i. 270).

awoke weak and unrefreshed. I meant to have been out by five to get my regiment off to pursue the enemy; but it was near six before I got to them, and then found Major Baker, the military director, fuming at them for not being ready. I did all I could, but it was hopeless. My chiefs called the men : they would do nothing—their breakfasts were cooking, and they would not hurry. I had not the strength to do more, and got as many as I could to the place they were to assemble in, and left them. Some officers were to go with them, and I hope they won't be afraid to follow a flying enemy. I then joined the General and his Staff, and returned with them to Cape Coast, and mercifully they gave me a hammock. I was nearly roasted in it, for the heat now is quite enough for anybody, and it was a weary journey, but the end was most exciting. My hammock was about the last, and just as I came near the town, the captured drum and chief trophies passed before me. The streets were crowded with women and what few men were left; and they shouted, and said all kinds of pretty things, if I had only understood them. I found myself entering in a triumph, like a Roman Emperor. I bowed and smiled, and waved my hand, and the women shouted and gesticulated; and this lasted all the way to Government House. Of course the General got the same; but the drum and myself certainly had a large share. I didn't object, for I knew I had worked hard for these poor creatures against those devils.

The letter goes on to give rather a miserable account of the doings of his native contingent after he left them. Sir Garnet was disposed to disarm them, and turn them into labourers, but he asked Mr. Marshall to have another try at them. The following official letter was received about this time :

Head Quarters, Cape Coast,
Nov. 13*th*, 1873.

Sir,—I have the honour, by direction of H.E. the Major-General Commanding, to thank you for the services recently rendered by you in connection with the Cape Coast Native Allies, and at the same time to express to you his appreciation of the trouble taken by you in going into the field with these men, attended, as it must have been, with much discomfort.

As, however, these levies have shown themselves to be utterly worthless in the field, the Major-General has therefore determined on converting the bulk of them into carriers, and would accordingly feel much obliged if you would proceed to Beulah to-morrow, the 14th inst., and communicate to Chief Attah and the whole of the Cape Coast Native Allies present in camp the instructions of H. E. the Governor which are contained in a letter attached.

I have the honour to remain,
Sir,
Your obedient servant,
L. D. BAKER, Major,
Acting Chief of the Staff.

The Hon. Judge Marshall, Cape Coast.

The letter of instructions was to the effect that only four hundred of the native contingent were to retain· their arms, and the rest were to be employed as carriers; and if any of these latter deserted, his place would be supplied by one of the four hundred.

Mr. Marshall's meeting the chiefs at Beulah, where he held a court and with the full consent of the chiefs, passed certain stringent but necessary enactments, was misrepresented by *The Times'* correspondent; but the conduct of the Judge is sufficiently vindicated in the following extract from a minute of Sir Garnet Wolseley:

I felt I could not allow all further military operations to be brought to an end until I had tried what coercion could effect. I had exhausted all other means for obtaining the carriers I required, so coercion alone

remained to be tried. The Chief Magistrate, from whom
I received every assistance upon all occasions during this
trying time, in his capacity as Judicial Assessor, assembled the native Assessor's court of chiefs at Beulah,
and passed an ordinance, stating that it was the bounden
duty of all men belonging to the tribes in alliance with
Her Majesty to turn out during the war, and render all
and every assistance in their power in any capacity that
they might be called upon to act. Strengthened with
the power thus legally and with the consent and desire
of the chiefs conferred upon me, I directed Lieutenant-
Colonel Colley . . . to adopt coercive measures. . . . These
measures were crowned with complete success, and I
obtained the carriers necessary for my operations north
of the River Prah.[1]

It must be remembered that the Ashanti War
was entered upon solely for the defence of the
tribes on the coast under our protection against
the incursions of the Ashantis, who would, had
the British Government abandoned them, have
reduced them to slavery, and used them as victims
in their human sacrifices. Every facility was
promised to the Ashantis and other tribes in the
interior to reach the coast for purposes of trade,
but they could not be allowed to enslave or
massacre the weaker tribes who were relying on
the protection of England.

Accra, Nov. 23rd.—I had a solemn interview yesterday
with about the biggest King in the Protectorate, a real
genuine warrior, head of a fighting people. Their country
is Akim, next to the Ashantis, with whom they are
always deadly enemies. He came in to join Captain
Glover and the Accra tribes; as he had fought in the
beginning of the year with the Fantis, and found they
ran away and left him in the lurch. When he came,
Captain Glover was gone, so we exhorted him to return

---

[1] Brackenbury, *Ashanti War*, ii. 283, 284.

and assist the General in attacking the Ashantis as they retreated. His army has returned, but he has an immense following here with him. I thought they would never end : chiefs, captains, followers, slaves—in they trooped, but still, no King, until I saw two big swords or scimetars coming, and then I knew he was at hand. These are held in front of him, with his pipe-bearer, and another holding a rhinoceros'-tail to drive away flies, I think. He is evidently annoyed at his position here, and he said he would return and assist the General. But, of course, he has difficulties—no native can do anything quickly— and he declared he must wait for a reply from Captain Glover, as he had sent him a letter by a sword-bearer.

The Ashanti War drew the attention of the public to the Gold Coast, and *The Times'* correspondent made some very damaging statements about Judge Marshall, on account of his action as Assessor to the Native Chiefs. Two slave girls had been decoyed away from their master by some of the Houssas who were assisting our troops ; and by an order from the Judge they had been arrested on board the ship in which they had embarked, and brought back bound to Cape Coast. The incident was represented as a flagrant enforcement of the worst evils of slavery, and caused much indignant comment at home. Yet it was the duty of the Judge, not to alter the law, but to carry it out ; and Sir Garnet Wolseley thoroughly approved of Mr. Marshall's action, as he knew the circumstances, and of the personal grudge which prompted the reports. Lord Kimberley thought it necessary to ask for a full explanation, and also for Mr. Marshall's views upon the slavery question generally. He sent a carefully weighed report to the Colonial Office, and writes home, December 21, 1873 :

My great anxiety as Judicial Assessor has been to
protect slaves and women from cruel or unfair treatment,
and the court is sometimes half-full of them coming to
me. This morning, I had a man fined £5 for accusing
a slave girl of theft wrongfully. It was out of kindness
to the women on board the steamer that I summoned
them, as much as because I was really bound to do it,
on account of this domestic slavery being recognized
and adjudicated upon in my court. They were leaving
a comfortable home, to go with these Houssas through
the campaign, and then to be cast off, when they left
for their station, which is Lagos. It may be taken, put
together with my Beulah order for forcing men to work,
and I may be held up as a brute, without an opportunity
of defending myself. I must take my chance, and I
have plenty of friends here. Sir Garnet came in, as
I was busy consulting with two of the Staff, and laughingly
said, "Ah, Judge, you will be hanged for this," in a
manner by which I knew he would stick by me. In
all the Blue Books about the Gold Coast, the Judicial
Assessor's court is alluded to as exercising jurisdiction
over slavery, and as having done much to soften and
ameliorate it, which I am sure is my object.

Mr. Marshall's official account of the incident
was as follows :

A day or two after the detachment of Cape Coast
Houssas was sent from thence to Accra, to join Captain
Glover's expedition, a number of women and children,
both Houssas and Fantis, were sent on board one of the
mail steamers to be conveyed to Accra, to join the
Houssas. After they were on board, one of the principal
native ladies of the place came to me with the complaint
that two of her women-servants or domestic slaves had
run away from her and been received in the Houssa
barracks, and were then on board the steamer, taking
some of her property with them.
One of the most important duties of the Judicial
Assessor's court since its foundation, and which has been
constantly recognized in Committees of the House of
Commons on West African affairs, has been the regula-

tion, as far as it has been possible, of the system of what is called domestic slavery, which exists among all the tribes which compose the British Protectorate. This duty involves the recognition of the rights of the masters, as well as the protection of the servants.

The complaint of the lady was formally laid before me, and these women were being conveyed away from their mistress and town at the Government expense, and under charge of a colonial officer. They were leaving their mistress in a most improper manner, and throwing away a home where they were happy and comfortable, to become the servants and mistresses of Houssas in a dangerous campaign, at the end of which they would probably be cast adrift. I therefore issued a summons for them to appear before me in the Judicial Assessor's court. It is utterly untrue that there was any order or warrant for them to be dragged back into slavery. It was done in order to investigate the case. The summons was executed by the police on board the steamer; and when on board, they were violently assaulted, and their clothes torn by some of the women there, but according to the evidence of the police, neither of these two women offered any resistance.

When the two women appeared before me, I informed them why they had been brought back; and inquired of them whether they had any complaint of ill-treatment or unkindness to make against their mistress, who was not present, assuring them that it was my duty to protect them, if such was the case. They stated they had no complaint to make against her, and that they felt they had done wrong in leaving her as they had, and that they were willing to return to her, which they did without any compulsion whatever. And so the matter ended.

The second statement to the effect that "a wretched female slave was carried through the streets of Cape Coast bound hand and foot, that she was then endeavouring to escape from slavery, *and being under due legal process* carried back to her master," has no foundation whatever. Had any such treatment of any woman whatever been proved before me, I should have most certainly punished the guilty parties.

Colonel Brackenbury bears the following testimony to the assistance given to the expedition by the Judge :

The Chief Magistrate, Mr. Marshall, proceeded to Dunquah and reported thence that he was convinced the question of the nature of food had something to do with the desertion of the carriers, recommending that markets for the sale of *cankey* should be set up at as many of the stations as possible; but at the same time he wrote : " The main cause, however, of the wholesale desertion is simply the idle disposition of the natives : they hate work, and seldom do any, and to go suddenly in for carrying loads is too much for their feelings, patriotic or otherwise. The enemy being over the Prah must also be a great inducement to their retiring habits." The Chief Magistrate rendered invaluable service at Dunquah, as Captain Lees had done at Cape Coast : both of these gentlemen threw themselves heart and soul into the cause of the expedition, and worked with a zeal and energy above all praise.[1]

Mr. Marshall's own account to his mother is :

Dunquah, Jan. 9th, 1874.—I am again in camp, not this time against the Ashantis, but against our own people or supposed allies. It is impossible to invade Ashanti without a proper amount of food, and at present it is found impossible to get the natives to carry up one quarter of the amount required, in fact more food is required at Prahsu each day than comes in, and there are masses of stores here and at other places which cannot be carried up. I was kept at it all day on Sunday in the hot sun, consulting and acting, and on Monday I had a string of letters, which made me determine to go up country, to see if I could be of any use. I planned to go on that evening, but the bout of sickness left me too much done up. On Tuesday, at 6 p.m., I started in a hammock, and got to the first military station, called Inquabim. The Harmattan wind came on, and it was

---

[1] Brackenbury's *Ashanti War*, vol. ii. p. 29.

quite cool. Here I found some fellows on the way up, and so I determined to remain there for the night, and go on early with two others. The military camps are very luxurious compared to what I have had before, and I slept in a nice thatched bamboo hut. At 4 a.m. we turned out, and had some hot coffee, and then we set off for a moonlight march. But I was not up to the march, and had to use the hammock a great deal. We passed Assayboo, the furthest place I had been to, and then all was new to me. At Akroful we found the first detachment of the 23rd, and breakfasted there. On inquiry after the goat that walks in front of the Welsh regiment, we found it had died at the end of the first march. We then went on through lovely forest country, with beautiful flowers and creepers, and the morning kept fresh and cool. On arriving here, I was glad to find my old friend Colonel Festing in command, as I thought he had gone on to the front. . . . After getting here, the heat became tremendous. I have not felt it so hot before, and not a breath of wind. I again collapsed, and lay in a tent this time, in an almost apoplectic state. I again became sick, which relieved me, but I was fit for nothing until the cool of the evening came on, when I joined Festing and the others in the mess-hut. . . . I have had a gathering of kings, and Colonel Festing told them the serious state of affairs. They did not move a muscle, and I could have flogged them. I have a Prince to try for preventing carriers coming, and also a more ordinary being; but the witnesses are absent. *My* powers, however, cannot do much to meet the crisis. It is now a carrier war with our own allies, and the West India regiments are being employed under white officers to scour the country, to *seize* people, and even if necessary to burn their villages. The expedition is at a stand-still.

The importance of the matter may be gathered from the following letter from Sir Garnet Wolseley:

Camp Prahsu, Jan. 10*th*, 1874.

MY DEAR JUDGE,—Many thanks for your letter. Leave no stone unturned to get carriers. If any of Mr. J.

D

Earboles' company is near you, perhaps you might employ his officers to hunt up men. I will give any native so employed £10 for every one hundred carriers he brings, provided the carriers remain with us for sixty days. The post is just starting. Money is of no object, if we can only get carriers.

Very truly yours,

G. J. WOLSELEY.

The difficulty was at last surmounted, and the next letter is dated :

Cape Coast, Jan. 23*rd,* 1874.—Thank God I am back again in my verandahs, with the fresh sea-breezes blowing about me. On the morning of the 21st I was up early, as soon as it was light, and having had some breakfast, said good-bye to my camp friends, and set off for Akroful. . . . Yesterday morning I got up very early, and feeling quite fresh I declined a hammock freely offered me. I got on very well and met with troops upon troops of Cape Coast women and girls carrying loads; and as I gave them a hearty good morning, they gave a chorus of "Ahoora, ahoora," meaning "your servant," or "your slave," mingled with "morning, thank you, how do, good-bye," and any scraps of English they knew, their bright eyes and teeth glistening with laughing pleasure. They are by no means an ugly race in their features, and their figures are often perfect, only sadly disfigured by the bustle affair behind. There are no big blubber lips here. The inevitable baby sitting behind has generally a most comically sage look, and crying seems by no means their habit.

I have just had a letter from Maurice. Sir Garnet and his Staff, and I suppose the Rifle Brigade, crossed the Prah on the 20th, and he writes from a place called Akrofuma, dated the 21st. Part is official, saying that my convicts will be sent down here till the General returns. . . . I cannot help feeling relieved that the General has not ordered my convicts to be shot. The last trial was a chief, a fine big man; but proof was strong against him of having helped his people and

deserters to escape from the soldiers sent for them.
When the decision of guilt was given by the kings and
chiefs, and confirmed by me, after thinking it well over,
I summoned them all to the most central and open place
of the camp. They and their followers were ranged on
one side; on the other all the officers in the camp.
Behind were crowds of natives. I sat on a chair at the
opposite end to where the chief was brought. He stood
firm and erect as I passed the sentence on him, with his
cloth thrown over him, so like a *toga*, that he reminded
me strongly of some of the old Roman statues in the
Vatican. He never flinched, and walked away quite
composedly. I said all I could for him in my official
(letter) to Sir Garnet; and when he comes here, I will
take care to let him have means of communicating with
his people, to get them to present themselves as carriers.

It is satisfactory to learn from Colonel Brackenbury that

The extreme penalty of the law was not, however, in
any case inflicted; but the delinquents were kept under
sentence until the expedition was over.[1]

The same writer perfectly agrees with Judge
Marshall's opinion of the superiority of the Fanti
women as compared with the men.

The women have none of the indolence and cowardice
of the men; they are bright, cheerful, and hard-working,
and we got excellent service willingly performed by
them. They were amenable to discipline, and seemed
to possess the instinct of order. They possessed wonderful strength; and it was no uncommon sight to see a
woman carrying a load of ammunition or box of rice
on her head weighing between 50lb. and 60lb., with a
child of two years' old carried on the hump which they
wear behind. The women are not beautiful, though
sometimes, when they are quite young, there is a bright-
ness in their look that makes up for lack of good

[1] *Ashanti War*, vol. ii. p. 30.

features. Our little friend who gave us the first news of the evacuation of Mampon was good-looking in her way. So, too, was that poor Commendah girl who so barely escaped with her life at Abrakrampa.[1]

The services of Mr. Marshall were not only acknowledged by the letters and official minutes of the Commander-in-Chief, but he received in due time the Ashanti medal by special despatch. These details are recorded here in order to show more clearly the character of the people with whom his lot was cast, as well as for the insight they gave into the brave, cheery, and kindly spirit that rose superior to the depressing influences of that climate, which Colonel Brackenbury says is "deadly to European life."[2]

[1] *Ashanti War*, vol. ii. p. 322.   [2] *Ib.* p. 351.

CHAPTER III.

RELIGION IN WEST AFRICA.   FETISHISM.
WESLEYAN MISSIONS.   CATHOLIC MISSIONS.

MR. MARSHALL always maintained that, however bad the climate of the Gold Coast may be, much of the fatal effects of it were caused by the imprudence of Europeans who went there. Very temperate and regular habits enabled him to battle with it for nearly ten years. But the climate was not the worst drawback of the place to a Catholic. The spiritual desolation of the country afflicted him deeply.

For a man of his warm sympathetic temperament to be cut off from all the external means of grace, from all access to a priest, and with the prospect of dying without the sacraments, was a very severe trial. In his younger days he used to be spoken of by his friends as one who "enjoyed his religion," and hence to be cut off from its influences was a privation which he felt keenly. He felt that it was injurious to him spiritually, and exposed him to temptations to recklessness and indifference.

Even in the midst of the excitement of war, his Catholic heart grieved bitterly over the spiritual darkness of the land in which his lot was cast.

He wrote to an old friend, a Redemptorist Father,
the Rev. T. Livius :

Cape Coast, December 17*th*, 1873.—Your letter was a
great pleasure to me ; it was not only so interesting in
itself, but it was pleasant to hear a Catholic voice
speaking to me once more, in a land where heathenism
still prevails, and Christianity may be said to be non-
existent, unless in forms and shapes that seem to do
more harm than good. Having got on this subject, let
me express to you the sorrow and indignation I—and I
can answer for the other Catholics who are, or have been
here—feel at this vast English Protectorate, with so many
towns occupied by the English, being left without a
Catholic mission or one Catholic priest. Even on this
expedition, for which so many soldiers have volunteered,
a great number Irish, though I don't know what their
religion is—these have volunteered in crowds. A fleet of
men-of-war is here, and the sailors and marines co-
operate on shore, engineers, control men, artillery—every
branch of the service except cavalry are here, or are
coming—ready to face the double enemy of Ashantis
and climate. Sickness and death have done plenty of
work already, and will do more ; and it is impossible but
that there are many Catholics among them. And yet I
hear of neither priest nor Sister of Mercy having offered
to risk themselves for these men. I know of one Catholic
officer who died after going through the war in the early
part of the year; two others left dangerously ill; another
was so but the other day : how many more Catholics
there may be, I cannot tell. . . . There is a Vicaire
Apostolique, I believe, and certainly missionaries at Free
Town, capital of Sierra Leone, a fat, comfortable, lazy
place, where I should think there was but little to do.
There are missionaries and Sisters on the other side at
Lagos, a wealthy, flourishing young town. But here lies
the Gold Coast, with its towns, and villages, and tribes
up the Prah, all ready and open for civilization and improvement; and not a Catholic mission is, or ever has
been here, since the Portuguese possessed it for the sake
of selling the people as slaves.

One of the first things Sir Garnet Wolseley said to me was, to express his wonder that there were no Catholic missions on the coast ; and I don't suppose he can have known that I was a Catholic. One of the most experienced colonial officers, who is here for the present emergency, and who is as devoid of any Christian belief as any one that I ever met, has repeatedly said to me how he wished the Jesuits would come here in force, for he knew of their powers to improve the people by what he had seen in Jamaica. And yet the only missionaries are the Wesleyans, who, to their honour be it said, had chapels and missions scattered all over the country, but now destroyed by the Ashantis, except in the fortified places. And now there are the Dutch towns and provinces added to our rule—Elmina, with its castles, monuments of slavery, and warnings of the atonement which the *Catholic* nations owe to these poor natives. If no priests or Sisters are on their way, it is too late now for them to join the expedition, though there are plenty of hospitals preparing in Cape Coast, as well as several already pretty full. But if it be true that the Catholic Church is Catholic as regards the territorial world—which it is uncommonly difficult to believe in Africa,—surely at all events, some missions ought to be established on the Gold Coast. I forgot to say that at Accra, a flourishing town in the east, there are German Lutheran missionaries, as well as Wesleyans, who do much to elevate the people by education and teaching them trades. The Jesuits are being turned out of Europe, and so you tell me are the Redemptorists from Germany : here is a grand opening for them, and if the missions are only carried out on a large scale, sufficient to impress the native mind, as well as to secure proper care for the health of the missionaries, I believe they will succeed rapidly, as far as success is possible among niggers. And the road is about to be opened to the interior tribes beyond. Soldiers and merchants are all eager for it ; but where is the Christian missionary? It is not preaching and converting that is so much wanted just now, as to get hold of the natives' confidence and affections, to raise them from their present degradation, their miserable houses and habits, and to educate the *children*. It is what the Jesuits have done already in heathen lands. Here is another ground opening for them.

I did not think I was going to say so much on this head, but I am glad to relieve myself a little. One thing more I will say: That missionaries who could cultivate the ground, and trade a bit, would not only pay their way, but make money. The Basle missions get large funds from theirs in the East. If men come out without preparations, and trusting to alms, they will simply die, and effect nothing. Capital is necessary to make a real and an impressive start. Land may be cleared anywhere, and temporary bamboo houses built. The Church of England is represented by one nigger chaplain here, enormously paid, who reads the service on Sunday to a few people, and cannot even show schools for the money spent. I expect he will soon be disestablished.

The religion of the various tribes on the Gold Coast is generally known by the name of Fetish, and consists mainly of a grovelling fear of evil spirits, whom they endeavour to propitiate by various incantations, and especially by human sacrifices. Sir James Marshall says:

There is a horrible catholicity and unity in the belief which everywhere prevails, that after death the free man remains free, and that the slave remains a slave in the service of the spirit of whatever master he belongs to. It therefore follows, that the free man after death requires slaves in accordance with his rank and wealth when alive, and that slaves are sent to him by his family and dependents as an attention and mark of respect which would bring down serious punishment and calamity if neglected.[1]

Some idea may be formed of the enormous number of slaves thus sacrificed from the following words of Colonel Brackenbury:

[1] *Missionary Crusade in Africa*, p. 10.

Our principal medical officer, Dr. Mackinnon, was quartered at Coomassie in the house of the King's executioner, who paid him a visit on the night of our arrival, and told him that every day he killed two or three people; that he thought he killed at least a thousand a year, and that the number which he had killed in the week preceding our arrival was so great, that he could not tell how many victims he had slain.[1]

Christianity has, unfortunately, been presented to these poor heathen in anything but a satisfactory form. The first to occupy the stations on the coast were the Portuguese; and though they brought Catholic priests with them, and their missionaries have left traces of their work far into the interior of the Dark Continent, yet the main object of their coming was to procure slaves for their colonies in America, and thus they became identified with that odious traffic. And then, under the sinister influences of the notorious Pombal, they expelled the Jesuits, their most successful missionaries, from all their dominions, and cut at the root of their influence as a Catholic nation. Still, the only Catholics on the Gold Coast are the descendants of slaves who had been converted and liberated by the Portuguese. The Dutch, who succeeded them, did their utmost to destroy all Catholicity that the Portuguese left behind them. England has given the various sects by which she is divided at home every facility for propagating their peculiar notions in Africa. The respectable orthodoxy of the Established Church does not seem to have taken any hold on the African people. But the Wesleyan Methodists, with their

---

[1] *Ashanti War*, ii. 339.

rollicking hymns and noisy revival meetings,
appear to have attracted a considerable number of
the negro population to their ranks. Colonel
Brackenbury says :

> The Wesleyan mission is apparently the only one
> which has gained any footing about Cape Coast, . . .
> whether they have really done any work of advantage,
> the writer had no fair opportunity of judging. . . . So
> far as we could judge from the specimens of native
> Christians sent to us from Sierra Leone, the missionary
> work had not been a success. A Sierra Leone native is
> great at going to church, and has his mouth full of sacred
> quotations, but he is generally as specious a knave as
> ever breathed. The Basle mission, which has its chief
> station at Akropong, in the Aquapim Hills, appears to
> have done some really good work. Captain Glover's
> testimony to the behaviour of the native Christians under
> his command is one that says much for these devoted
> missionaries. But this mission is in reality a large trading
> establishment, and it combines the teaching of industrial
> habits and honest labour with inculcation of the Christian
> virtues and the principles of the Christian religion.[1]

Sir James Marshall, after nine years' experience,
tells the same tale of the results of Wesleyan
teaching upon the natives :

> The Methodist gave them the Bible, and taught them
> to read of polygamy, concubinage, and other things in
> the Old Testament which 'suited them exactly, coupled
> with bellowing hymns about salvation free, and without
> labour or trouble, which gave everything a sanctimonious
> finish, and created a miserable imitation of Christianity
> which, I often thought, made the poor heathen worse than
> he was before. The Jewish Sabbath, ordained by God
> to be kept on the seventh day of the week, but grafted
> by Protestantism on to the Sunday, or Lord's day of the
> Catholic Church, suited the negro equally with other

things he read about in the Old Testament. The negro delights in being told he must rest and do no work. He would like six Sabbath-days to one day of work.[1]

After a time, the hopes expressed by Mr. Marshall in the letter quoted at the beginning of this chapter were partially satisfied by the arrival of the Rev. A. Wallace, an English priest, who volunteered to accompany the troops. He remained at Cape Coast for some little time, saying Mass at first at the house of the Chief Magistrate, and afterwards in a room in the town. He collected a band of Catholics around him, and if he could have stayed would doubtless have effected much good. A difficulty, however, occurred in consequence of there being no Catholic Bishop in the British territory. The whole of this coast has hitherto been left to the care of the French Society of African Missions, which has its head-quarters at Lyons. With every wish to spend themselves generously for the souls of these poor Africans, lack of numbers and means compelled this devoted body of men to leave large districts entirely unprovided for. And as they were entrusted with the responsibility of the whole coast, it was impossible for them to exercise proper authority over a priest who did not belong to their Society. There were difficulties in the way of Father Wallace becoming a member of the Society, and therefore, to his own regret, and still more to the regret of the Catholics on the Gold Coast, he had to return to England.

After the Ashanti War, the affairs of the Gold Coast were put upon a more systematic footing. A regular judicial system was established, and

[1] *Reminiscences*, p. 10.

Mr. Marshall, after his well-earned six months'
leave, was transferred to Lagos as puisne Judge.
Lagos is at the eastern extremity of the British

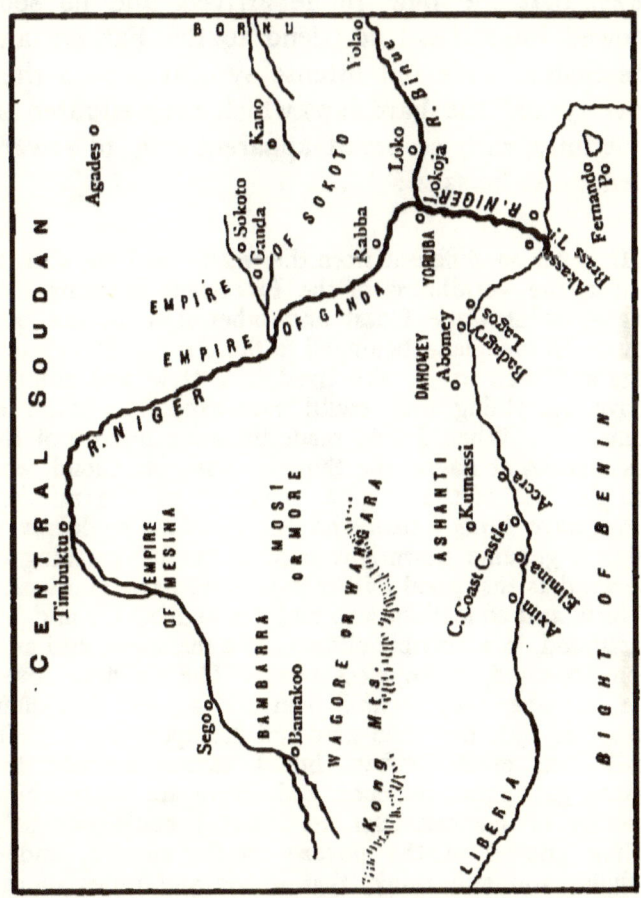

possessions, and is separated from the Gold Coast
by the Kingdom of Dahomey, and is the most
flourishing trading-station in that part of Africa.
Here there had been for ten years a Catholic
mission, served by the Fathers from Lyons.   There

was also a convent, and French nuns, who at that time could not speak English. It was in January, 1875, that the new Judge arrived, and he soon showed himself a true friend to the Fathers and the Sisters. He felt intense sympathy with their poverty and the hardships which they endured so cheerfully, with so small apparent fruit to reward them. As he says :

It is all so different from the wealth and comfort, as well as the worldliness of the Protestant missions. At Lagos, as at Cape Coast and other stations, the best houses in the place belonged to the Protestant missionaries and their wives, who lived in a style and comfort above everything they could ever expect to attain at home. . . . When I first made the acquaintance of the missionaries at Lagos, the Superior was Père Cloud, who was the last of the original members of the mission. Never have I met a man who impressed me so deeply as being a genuine downright saint in the full meaning of the word as that good Father did. Here was a gentleman of birth and education, who had devoted his life and his priesthood, in a horrible climate, to a thankless, and as it then appeared, a hopeless work. The children loved him, but when they became men and women, they often gave him little else than pain and disappointment. His health was much broken, but I cannot describe the beauty, gentleness, patience, and above all, the touching humility of his character. . . . But I could not help feeling grieved at the poverty of the mission, and I thought, and still think, that if the authorities of the Propaganda had realized the importance and advantages of West Africa in a missionary point of view, the missions would have been more numerous and better supported. Large sums have been spent on comparatively hopeless and useless missions, whilst those of West Africa have been starved, and are so still.[1]

[1] *Reminiscences*, pp. 19, 20.

In 1876, he wrote to a priest friend about this good Father :

The mission here is very poor, and has all Africa before it, and I think my principal duty lies there. The poor Padres have a hard time of it, and I fear very little fruit falls to them. The only hold the Catholic Church seems to have is upon the families of the emancipated slaves of Brazil and Cuba, who also form the most industrious portion of the Lagos community. The Principal of the mission has been very dangerously ill : very near death. I know it will please you to hear that I was with him daily, and that in his delirium he asked for me, and refused to see the doctor until he was told I had asked him to do so. He was then ordered home, and I was the person to tell him, and to assure him that he really must go. Seldom have I felt so much respect and admiration for a man as for this Father Cloud, and his patience and gentleness in his weary work, which has lasted for some fifteen years out on this coast ; getting many an insult and rebuff from the French and Portuguese so-called Catholics, but generally Freemasons and Communists. You may imagine therefore my surprise and pleasure, when I found that in his illness he turned to me in the way he did, and on leaving declared my visit had saved his life. It is indeed a blessing to be in a position where I am of some real use in the world, and am helping towards the civilization of a vast country.

Of another missionary he writes :

Père Louàpre was a most charming man and an admir-able missionary who had been an army chaplain in Algeria. He arrived soon after I did, with, I think, two others. Shortly after his arrival I found him located in a small ground-floor room, used for keeping stores, suffering from an attack of fever, after a night of rain, which came through the roof, and forced him to sit up on his bed under an umbrella. His description of his sufferings and inconveniences was most amusing and comical. Every-thing was turned into a joke, mixed with laughing protes-tations that his missionary vocation did *not* include living

in a store-room with a leaky roof, which forced him to
sit up in bed under an umbrella, instead of lying down to
sleep. Happily before long the mission-house was finished,
with a set of well-ventilated rooms on the first floor, and
the Fathers moved into it. The event was celebrated by
a dinner, at which I was one of the few guests, and a
merry, happy gathering it was. . . . These French Fathers,
in addition to their missionary character, afforded a most
charming society in a part of the world where pleasant
and superior society is very scarce, and no amount of
fevers, troubles, and disappointments ever crushed the
spirit or zeal of those noble, good men.[1]

These good Fathers could be very firm when it
was necessary to maintain the discipline of the
Church. The following incident shows what the
Church has to suffer from the evil influence of
Freemasonry, even in those distant places. Sir
James writes :

Not long before I arrived, a Portuguese merchant died
without the sacraments, a Freemason, as well as a notorious evil liver. He was rich and popular, especially
among the Freemasons, and he was a Catholic, and had
been tolerably generous in gifts to the Church. . . . He
died a Freemason, unreconciled to the Church, and
whilst he left the poor man's soul to be judged by God,
Père Cloud steadily and firmly refused Christian burial
to his body. . . . This refusal to bury a man of position
and importance roused the fury and indignation of the
Freemasons and their friends. . . . They had not yet
adopted the open denial of any God, which is the boast
of many Freemason lodges, in addition to the entire
ignoring of Christianity and the Christian's God which
prevails in all, and therefore they could not bury him
with atheistic or pagan rites of their own as is now done
in France by the Masons. But Père Cloud remained
firm, and showed that however humble and poor the
Church was in its earthly circumstances, its spiritual
authority and power was from God. The Protestant

[1] *Reminiscences*, pp. 20, 21.

ministers, at the same time, proved how very opposite their position was, for they were only too pleased to receive the weed thrown out of the Pope's garden, and buried the excommunicate outcast as one who ought to have belonged to them.

As the deceased had no relations in Lagos, his property was placed by my predecessor in the hands of another Portuguese, a man of the same stamp, and a strong Freemason. Of course his duty was to administer the estate for the heirs at law. After some time the heirs applied to the court for information about the property, as they had received nothing, nor any accounts. It therefore became my duty to examine into the affair, which ended in my making out a warrant for the apprehension of this precious friend of the deceased, on the charge of having appropriated everything he could lay hold of to his own use. But his brother-Masons got wind of it, and though I did all I could to have him arrested, they managed to smuggle him out of the jurisdiction in a canoe, and had no hesitation in acknowledging they had done so. So I learned that the fraternity of Freemasonry included fraternity in crime, and that even when a Mason robbed the property of a brother-Mason he was protected by his brethren from the law. This man's hatred of Père Cloud and the priests was something extraordinary, such as seems to exist only in the heart of bad Catholics who have renounced, without really losing, their faith.[1]

It is not to be wondered at that these Freemasons made many attempts to persuade Mr. Marshall to join their society. He laughed at them, and told them that he knew all about them, as, when he was an undergraduate at Oxford, he had, with several of his young friends, been initiated, and even been made a "Master Mason;" but had renounced it all when he became a Catholic. They were obliged to confess that he

[1] *Reminiscences*, pp. 21—23.

spoke the truth ; and this made them hate him, almost as much as they hated the Fathers.

Mr. Marshall felt very strongly, as an English Catholic, that while the Gold Coast belonged entirely to England, and there was every facility for English missions afforded by the Government, yet all the Catholic missionary work was being done by the French ; and the interest and money of English Catholics was diverted from a part of the continent of Africa which had special claims upon them, and given to heroic but disastrous expeditions into the interior, where there was every opportunity for martyrdom, but small prospect of establishing any hold on the natives. On the Gold Coast the fields were ripe for the harvest, and yet the Wesleyans were left to reap it. After many attempts to stir up his Catholic friends by private letters, he make a public appeal in the *Tablet*, in June, 1877, in which he said :

Everything that is being done in the way of Catholic missions in these English colonies is by France, which supplies the priest, the Sisters, and the most part of the money. On the whole of the Gold Coast there is not a single Catholic priest or mission of any nation, and here at Lagos, it is the Society of African Missions at Lyons that is doing the work. . . . The only public church at present is the Sisters' reading-room, a plain oblong shed, with the earth for a floor. Sufficient progress has now been made to induce the Fathers to endeavour to build a church worthy of the name, and which will be the first of any mark in our West African settlements. They have prepared their plans, and are about to commence, in the hope that funds will be provided to enable them to finish it. Lagos is British territory, and is a flourishing port, increasing in importance and in population, European and native. . . . These good missionaries do

E

not get much assistance or encouragement to cheer them in their terribly hard and thankless task, and I know it will confer an immense pleasure upon them to receive some substantial recognition from England, the more so as French Catholics naturally feel that they are not called upon to assist an English colony as much as if it were their own. They have never asked anything from England, and they do not know that I am asking for them.

His appeal fell rather flat, for in May, 1880, he writes again :

At Lagos the missionaries for three years past have been struggling to build a decent church, which they have not yet been able to finish. An appeal was made through the *Tablet* to English Catholics at home to help these Frenchmen labouring in an English colony, with the result of one donation of £5 from a priest, and some church needlework from a servant girl.

This last letter was written with reference to the disasters which Bishop Comboni had narrated as having befallen the Central African Missions. Mr. Marshall says :

I honour and reverence Bishop Comboni and his band ; I honour and reverence their Christian heroism in being determined to carry on the Mission in Central Africa, which has already cost them so dear, but I do wish to be allowed, on behalf of places like this coast, to ask, Why is the centre not approached through coasts like this, where everything has for years been made ready for the Church to begin her labours ? From Sierra Leone on the extreme west, to the Bight of Benin and Lagos, there is not a Catholic priest or mission, though Protestant missions are established all along the coast perverting the natives by an indiscriminate reading of the Old Testament and a miserable parody of Christianity. The British Government has been established on the Gold Coast for very many years, and every encouragement is given to missionaries to build churches and schools, and civilize the people. Grants of money have increased, and land is easily got. The Government is carrying its power and influence into the interior, and, since the Ashanti War, communication is becoming more constant and frequent with the interior towards Timbuctoo. The Wesleyan and German Lutheran missions, established out here for fifty years past, are making use of all this, and, depend upon it, wherever they settle it will be much more difficult to establish the Faith, as Old Testament Christianity suits the negro nature far better than the Catholic faith.

The Gold Coast has now been placed by Propaganda under the French Missionary Society, which has charge of Lagos, and for six months past two priests have been expected at Elmina, where some traces of the Faith from Portuguese times still linger. But they have not come, and when they do, What are they to do in such a tract of country? Also, Frenchmen have the double disadvantage of having to speak English as well as the native language, for French is useless.

When any inquiries are made as to why missionaries are not sent here, the answer is, They go where Rome sends them. It may be presumptuous to say so, but it does seem strange, especially at a time when there is so much talk of opening up Africa, why a country like this, where missions can be established without opposition, where natives are still as heathen as in the interior, is so neglected. If a mission such as that which has been sent to Central Africa had been sent to the Gold Coast, there would have been as much for them to do as in the centre, without the same terrible suffering and loss, and when missions are established on the coast, a base of operations is found for the campaign in the interior.

Accra, April 24th.

This letter called forth a letter from Father Barrett, of St. Joseph's College, Cork, explaining how that College had been founded mainly by a Yorkshire gentleman, Thomas Himsworth, Esq., to meet the very many difficulties pointed out by

Mr. Marshall, and to send out English-speaking priests, trained for the African Mission by the same Society, whose head-quarters are at Lyons. On the 3rd of July, Mr. Marshall was able to write again :

I am glad to be able to tell you that two French priests belonging to the Society of African Missions, Lyons, have sailed and settled at Elmina, near Cape Coast Castle. There they have found two French Catholic merchants to welcome them, and they have been warmly received, not only by the English officers of the Government, but also by the Governor of the colony, Mr. Ussher, who happened to be there at the time of their arrival. I may add that an English man-of-war gave them a passage from St. Helena.

The *Tablet* of the 18th of September, in the same year, contains an interesting letter from Père Moreau, one of the Fathers mentioned, in which he gives an account of their reception at Elmina, and says :

After our arrival, we visited the old chiefs and the inhabitants of the town, and were kindly received everywhere.

All knew that we were about to arrive, and inquired when did we intend opening our schools. Yesterday the chief, Acra Coean, asked us if we should teach English and French ; he wished to send us some of his children that they may learn these languages, and could himself alone furnish us with scholars enough to form a numerous class, having no less than fifty boys. . . . We entertain hopes of being able to do much good here ; the population is favourable to us, the Wesleyans alone being hostile. All this part of the coast was, it is said, Catholic under the Portuguese dominion. Of this there are still some traces left ; for in all the houses that we visited we have found pictures, statues, &c., which are evidently Catholic emblems of the Saints. On Friday they celebrate a feast of our Lady, retaining in their language the Portuguese name "Santa Maria." Naturally, there were many superstitious ceremonies, fetichism, frequent tom-toms and war-dances, and, if I am not mistaken, a little inebriety. But it will be possible for us to correct these abuses, and bring back to their original simplicity these remains of Catholicism.

He goes on to give an account of their visit to the Governor, who received them very courteously, and said he was very glad to see them established there.

He knows our missions of Lagos and Porto Novo, and asked if we intended to open schools. I answered in the affirmative, adding that we wanted to found a kind of agricultural colony for teaching boys the art of tillage.

"If such is your intention," he replied, "train up gardeners; we have a few, and cannot do without them."

"I have seen," said I, "in the *St. Helena Gardens* that you want gardeners for the Gold Coast."

"It is true, but none offer themselves; I have even written to China in order to procure some from those parts."

"But for gardens, you want land."

"I will give you as much of it as you desire."

"Will you grant us what we ask?"

"Certainly, if the thing is at all possible."

"Could you give us the Dutch Garden?"

"It belongs to the English Government. I cannot dispose of it without their consent; ask for it, and I am here ready to support."

We could not but thank him from our hearts for his benevolence towards us. . . . The Dutch Garden is situated in a magnificent place, on a rising ground to the south-east of the town, about one hundred metres from the sea. It is planted with fruit-trees, has walks, channels, and a beautiful fish-pond in the centre, and is almost entirely surrounded by a wall. The Dutch used to take care of it; but since the English came into

possession it is not so well cared for as it used to be.
There we would have a garden very nearly in order, and
sufficient space for erecting some buildings.

They succeeded in getting this very eligible
piece of ground, but one of them, Père Murat,
fell a victim to the climate before they had been
at Elmina a month. Nothing daunted, Père
Moreau, who was soon joined by another priest,
Père Holley, and with him made an expedition to
Abeokuta, a place inhabited by some two hundred
thousand refugees from the cruelties of the King
of Dahomey. The principal King received them
gladly, in spite of the efforts of the Protestant
missionary to induce him to drive them away.
He gave them land in a very healthy situation,
and Père Holley remained to establish a mission
there. There was a small nucleus already, consisting of about twenty Catholic natives lately
returned from Brazil, and as soon as the school
was opened, Père Holley found himself surrounded
by ninety children. Another mission was also
commenced at Whydah, on the coast of Dahomey.
The next year Mr. Marshall wrote :

After an absence of two years, my duties took me to
Lagos this last Easter, and it was indeed gratifying to
see the great and substantial progress that had been
made. The Masses at both chapels were crowded, and
the number of communicants of both sexes was really
large. The good Fathers are at last beginning reaping
a harvest after the long years of thankless toil, and feel
that the mission is getting a real hold upon the country.
The schools received a great impulse from the occasional
arrival of an Irish Brother or Sister. Unhappily the
climate has been very particularly cruel to these good
Irish, and especially to the Sisters, but the work has
gone on.

Three years later, in 1884, Père Chausse, the Superior at Lagos, wrote to Sir James:

> Our missions are getting on well, and are developing under the blessing of God. In 1863, when our first Fathers arrived, there were three adults who performed their Easter duties. Last Easter we had nearly nine hundred communicants. The Mass is well attended. Christian marriages are held in honour, and the schools have given great satisfaction to the Government Inspector.

Great as was his zeal in the cause of African Missions, he held rather peculiar views about the general character of missionary literature. He had a great dislike to dismal stories of the sufferings undergone by missionaries, which dwelt exclusively upon the penitential side of the subject, and were too often unrelieved by those bright sparks of humour which reflect the happy spirit of Christian heroism. It has often been remarked, that the pictures painted by the early Christians in the Catacombs of Rome, during centuries of continual persecution, are all of a bright and joyous character, and breathe the spirit of peace and charity, and, except in very rare instances, pass by all allusion to suffering. It is well known that the most severe religious orders, where the greatest austerities are practised, are just those where the inmates seem basking in the sunshine of perpetual peace. The heroic life and death of Father Damien has called forth enthusiastic admiration from all, and that devoted priest tells us in one of his letters:

> Jesus Christ is in a special manner with missionaries. It is He Who in the midst of trials, contradictions, and

sufferings will cause us to enjoy a happiness of which
he who has never experienced it can form no idea. For
the graces of our state are so powerful that the greatest
difficulties and trials do not trouble us. We already
feel this, for when about to launch out into the midst
of a stormy ocean, not only are we free from fear (this
the sailors are), but we are as merry as can be. After
being half an hour together, we are often quite tired
with laughing and telling funny stories.[1]

And so James Marshall's own joyous temperament delighted in the cheerful light-hearted spirit
that he found so often among the missionaries
of the West Coast of Africa. In his *Reminiscences*
he says :

The usual idea of missionaries is, I think, that they
are melancholy men, living in misery and hardships,
always expecting to be eaten or treated in some dis-
tressing manner. And really missionary literature does
seem to give some ground for these suppositions. The
Annals of the Propagation of the Faith, and other missionary publications, seem to me in general too depressing
and dull, always giving the gloomy side of things, and
dwelling upon trials, dangers, and difficulties, and re-
velling in martyrdoms and cruelties. My own experience
is that I never had better company than that of the
missionaries at Lagos, and that they were as happy and
cheery a set of men as I ever met. Soldiers are ready
to go to any part of the globe, and if it is to war, with
its hardships, dangers, and risk of wounds and death,
they go amidst cheers and congratulations. Others like
myself go to bad climates or anywhere else for a living,
and to get on in life. The missionary has a far higher
vocation and aim, and so long as he is faithful to that
vocation his is by far the happiest lot. I cannot see
therefore why missionary narratives cannot be made a
little more cheerful and amusing. I never met a gloomy
or depressed character among the West African mission-

[1] *Life of Father Damien,* p. 48. Catholic Truth Society.

aries ; and when down with fever, or boils, or dysentery, or any other climatic miseries, they were still cheery and amusing. The pluck of a soldier made even the Ashanti Expedition a sort of amusing picnic to those who really had pluck, and they were decidedly the majority. So also the vocation of the missionary keeps him happy and cheerful through everything, and if this spirit prevailed more in missionary literature, I think it would take better with the general public. The letters I still get from my missionary friends are always amusing as well as interesting, and when troubles come upon them, they fall upon those who know and realize that they above all people are in the hands of the good God, whose soldiers and servants they are. I have seen them under almost every form of trial, but I never saw them give way to despondency. For a time, when I thought of their apparently wasted, hopeless work, I found it difficult to believe that Christianity could be intended for the negro of Africa. But they entertained no such thought, and have gone cheerily on, and I have given good proof that I was wrong in thinking so.[1]

Perhaps this extract will form the most fitting conclusion for this chapter, in which we have tried to put on record James Marshall's leading thoughts about Catholic African Missions.

[1] *Reminiscences*, pp. 33, 34.

CHAPTER IV.

OFFICIAL LIFE. VISIT TO KING OF PORTO NOVO.
MARRIAGE. MADE CHIEF JUSTICE. FAILURE
OF HEALTH. KNIGHTED. RETIREMENT.

IT seemed better to give James Marshall's thoughts
upon African Missions in a separate chapter, than
to keep to strict chronological order. We may
now take up the narrative of his life from the conclusion of the Ashanti Expedition.

The Ashanti medal was sent to him by special
despatch in consideration of his services, and when
he returned to Africa in 1875 he was transferred
to Lagos. His influence with natives induced the
Governor, Mr. Dumaresq, to ask him to undertake
a mission to the King of Porto Novo. The
account he sent home of this expedition is naturally more interesting than his official report, and
we therefore give the letter to his mother :

On Friday, June 18th, 1875, I received instructions
from the Administrator, Mr. Dumaresq, to hold myself
in readiness to proceed next morning to Porto Novo by
the s.s. *Ekuro*, to deliver a letter to the King of Porto
Novo, calling upon him to put an end to the custom of
human sacrifices. . . . The *Ekuro* is a new steamer
which came out only three days before, and is of a far
higher style than anything that has yet been here, and
it is really a pleasure to travel in her. At 1.30, on

Saturday the 19th, I went on board the *Ekuro*, which hoisted the Government ensign, with an interpreter and a guard of Houssa soldiers.   Mr. Hutchinson, the owner, was on board, and went with me, which made it much more pleasant. For two days there had been tremendous rains, but this day was beautiful : bright, but with clouds, and a fresh cool breeze.   I was delighted to find the little ship so comfortable and well-adapted to the tropics. The branch of the lagoon that stretches to Porto Novo lies to the westward, close to the sea all the way.   It is a narrow strip of land, seldom more than a quarter of a mile wide, that separates them.   It is much the same as a fine river, branching off occasionally in various directions, and at times widening out into quite a large lake. For a long time we saw nothing but mangroves on each side, which tell of swamps and fevers.   Occasionally a clump of cocoa-nut trees appeared, and under them a village was sure to be found, the huts consisting of bamboos with thatched roofs.   As we got further on, the scenery became more of a forest kind, principally composed of the oil, cabbage, and cocoa-nut palms ; but the country was everywhere flat.   Once we saw the ground rise perhaps to forty feet, and it was something to note. The navigation is very ticklish for a large vessel, and it is only by pilots who know the landmarks all the way that a vessel can be taken.   We had the man who was considered the best, rejoicing in the name of King John. He did very well, but unfortunately at one place became possessed with the idea that he would try if the *Ekuro* would go over a particular part, and the *Ekuro* objected. It was after sundown, and just as dinner was announced, and the soup was on the table, on looking over the side, to my horror I saw we were not moving.   I went and told Mr. Hutchinson, who was washing up for dinner, and out he came, naturally in a great state of mind. The engines never ceased, and the Houssas performed a violent dance on the fore-deck, so that the little ship could never settle down ; and after about twenty minutes or half an hour she worked her way through the obstruction, and we again went on. . . . At about eight o'clock we passed Badagry, the last post of the British territory,

where there is a commandant and a small force of
Houssas. Our whistle shrieked, and the people on shore
showed lights, and we further fraternized by burning blue
lights and sending up some rockets. It was a beautiful
moonlit night, and we sat on deck, smoking our pipes,
and thoroughly enjoying it all. A little before ten, we
found ourselves off Porto Novo, and on dropping anchor,
bang went our gun, followed by a rocket. Immediately
we could hear the inhabitants all talking together, making
a most queer noise. I should think everybody spoke at
once. Off went another rocket, producing an increased
swell of human sounds, and I got a little nervous as to
this display. Off went another, and then I begged it
might be stopped at once, or I might be charged with
bombarding the place. All was soon quiet again, and
we turned in. I had a swinging cot on deck, and
Mr. Hutchinson had a spring mattrass, and we were both
soon sound asleep. Unfortunately, I had an attack of
nightmare, which occasionally happens to me, and I
dreamed that I was being violently and fiercely attacked,
I suppose by the Porto Novians. The unlucky part of
it was that I gave vent to my feelings, as lustily as
though I really had been attacked, and my shouts
brought the steward to my assistance ; and I felt remarkably small when, on coming to myself, I found the
steward by my side assuring me it was all right, and that
I was safe in the middle of the stream. I had another
attack later on, and fancied the ship was sinking, and I
know I holloaed out, but to my great relief it attracted
nobody to my side this time.

On waking up on Sunday morning, we found the rainy
season had again prevailed, and all was dreary and wet,
with a thick misty rain. I took a look at Porto Novo,
and saw that the European houses were most of them
well away from the town, and upon what can almost be
called a hill, certainly the highest piece of ground I have
seen in this part of Africa, looking over a wide expanse
of lagoon, and even over the strip of land on the opposite
side on to the sea. The native town was, as usual, on
the lowest and most marshy part available, and seemed
just like all other African towns, a mass of houses built

of bamboo, or earth made into what is called "swish."
The only exception I have seen is Cape Coast, so long
the seat of British rule, where they have not advanced so
far as thatched roofs, but use flat roofs of swish, which
carefully catches the heavy rains and causes destruction
and slaughter whenever the rains are particularly heavy,
which is not seldom.

I despatched the interpreter to the King with my
compliments, and to tell him that I was the bearer of an
important letter, and should be glad if he would give me
an early interview.   I had very little expectation of his
fixing the same day, but the interpreter brought back
word that he would see me at ten o'clock.   This was
quite a surprise, and disarranged our breakfast plans.
I said I should prefer breakfast being delayed ; but at
the same time, as a British ambassador, I could not
meet a King on international subjects of vital importance on an empty stomach.   The steward said there was
some fish all ready.   I immediately said that was the
very thing, and so it was.   These sinners, stewards and
servants, had fish just out of the water, capitally cooked,
which we should never have seen or known of but for
the interposition of this royal summons. It was delicious,
and made me feel equal to any King or Prime Minister
—except Bismark.

The Houssas having landed, I and Mr. Hutchinson,
with our two boys and my orderly, followed, and happily
the rain ceased.   As we got near the shore, I said to
Mr. H., "Now we must do the dignified."   I speedily
found I had spoken too soon.   The boat was aground
some distance from anything like land, and there was
a considerable space of nasty swamp to be crossed.   Two
Houssas came to carry the ambassador on shore.   Now
with Kroo boys, who live in the water, I manage a crisis
of this sort very well.   Each takes a leg, and the only
difficulty that ever arises is that they sometimes have a
tendency to take different directions.   This is met by
holding tight one, and using strong language to the
other.   But the Houssas are not accustomed to the
thing, and carried me anyhow, and I was in an agony
lest that it would end in my being upset into the filthy

swamp. All my dignity vanished amidst the grins of the
assembled natives, and the worst of it was, the fellows
would not put me down when there was ground to stand
upon, and I began to fear that they thought they must
carry me all the way; but I shouted to the interpreter to
save me, and at last found myself on my legs.   Mr.
Hutchinson is a very big man, and it took three to carry
him, and he managed better by taking a horizontal
position, and being carried like a huge baby.

Having landed, we recovered our dignity, and the
procession formed. First the Houssas two and two,
followed by Mr. Willoughby, paymaster, and my interpreter; then our noble selves, followed by our boys and
my orderly. As we went along I was struck with the
universal nature of small boys, an increasing number of
whom followed upon our heels, making remarks doubtless as pungent as a London street-boy could make.
Porto Novo is not nice; and I must say this for the
towns on the Gold Coast that had the blessing of British
Government, that I never saw in any of them more filth
or smelt more horrible stinks than I did in that march
through Porto Novo. But the Europeans do not live in
the midst of it all, like they do in Cape Coast and Accra.

After a good long walk, we came to the royal palace.
Outside the gate there was a rough model of a hideous-
looking human head on the ground—some fetish.   The
outer wall of enclosure and all the buildings are of the
mud composition called swish, and this abode of royalty
looked as squalid and filthy as what one usually finds in
native establishments, royal or otherwise. On entering
the gate we found ourselves in an oblong courtyard, with
rooms opening into the piazza which runs round it, and
which was filled with a number of men and boys with
nothing on them but old and dirty-looking cloths round
their middles. The women seemed to be kept out of
sight. The court itself was exceedingly muddy after the
rains, and in the middle were three miniature huts containing various kinds of fetish, but I could make nothing
out of them as to what they were, except some more
ugly models of heads. Here two chairs were brought to
us, with a message from the King that he would see us

soon. So we sat down, and became the object of much contemplation and conversation among the royal household. Among them was a man with a very curiously-shaped sword, but very suggestive of cutting off heads, and I hinted to Hutchinson that perhaps we were about to test its capabilities.

Presently we were told that the King would be glad to see us, and we were ushered into an inner court, which happily was a great deal cleaner. Along the piazza on one side I saw a number of men seated on the ground, and more on the floor of the court opposite. I was at a loss, and said to the interpreter, " Which is the King?" " There, on the sofa," he replied. And so it was. He was wrapped all over in a sort of sheet made of Croydon, with a white cap on his head, lying full length on a very aged and well-worn European sofa. I at once made for him, and found him quite a young man, with an intelligent and exceedingly pleasant face. Having shaken hands, and interchanged compliments, we sat down. The nobility, who were there in force, had very seedy clothes on, and there was no sign of regal wealth or splendour. An attendant brought in a small table, with two tumblers and a caraffe of water. The interpreter told me the King could not speak to me until we had drunk something. The attendant filled the glasses, and to my surprise drank the contents, or part of them. I did not like the idea of water : in the first place, as there could be no filter there ; and still less did I like to drink after my sable brother had had a drink. But the interpreter told me that this was to show that there was no poison, and the glasses were rinsed out. We then drank, and a bottle of claret was produced, and we drank to the King's health. Then came business.

I read the letter sentence by sentence, telling the King that Her Majesty and her people are shocked when they hear of human sacrifices, and that the Governor had heard of the terrible atrocities that had lately taken place, when the King had sacrificed human beings in holding custom for his ancestors ; and that the British Government would not allow of such things. I looked as grave and stern as I could, and the interpreter had

thoroughly got up the letter, in order to give it its full
force; but I could not see a muscle move in any one
face of King or courtier, though they certainly looked
grave. I do not suppose they knew what was coming,
but they showed no sign of emotion. When I had
finished, I gave the letter to the King, and said that I
hoped he fully understood its meaning.

After a slight pause, the King's interpreter, who
conveys everything that is said to him, whether he
understands it or not, and who was in a prostrate but
reclining position at his feet, kissed the ground three
times in rapid succession, and spoke to him, and then
kissed the ground again. This kissing process was
repeated each time he spoke. A few of the chiefs also
made some remarks, and then the King addressed me.
He said it was true that there had been a sacrifice, but
the British Government had been misinformed about it.
If amongst us a man took a King's wife, what would be
done to him?

I replied that I expected that answer; and then, to
put on the screw, I said that I had served in the war
against the Ashantis, and had heard the messengers
from their King give exactly the same excuse for their
sacrifices.

He then said he loved his people, and did not like to
put them to death, but when they committed crimes he
had to do so; and that we had been misinformed, and
that if I would return at another time, he would tell me
the real truth of the matter.

I replied I could not do so, as my orders were to
return immediately.

He then said that the man who was sacrificed was a
criminal.

I replied that it was perfectly well known that it was
not one but many that were sacrificed, that they were
not criminals but slaves; and that it was well known
that human sacrifices were common in this part of Africa,
and that the British Government was determined to put
them down wherever it had the power to do so. I also
said I did not come there to argue the point, but that
the sacrifices must cease, and I was sure that in the

end he and his people would be glad that it should be so.

The King was now fairly in a corner, but kept perfectly composed, and now no longer made any subterfuges or denials, but said there should be no more.

To drive the nail quite home, I again said my message is, Human sacrifices must cease; and he replied that we should never hear of them again.

I think from what I saw and heard that the King will be pleased enough to keep his word, but it is difficult and dangerous for him to break down old customs, especially when connected with the fetish. He is not yet fully enthroned, and seems inclined to rule for himself.

Having finished this part of the business, which was the main object of my visit, I relaxed in tone of voice and severity of visage, and told him of a petition which the Government had received, complaining of the cruel and savage imprisonment of a Sierra Leone man. I was very cautious in what I said, and began by telling him that if Lagos people made disturbances in Porto Novo or broke his laws, he was quite right to punish them. The educated Sierra Leone natives are one of the chief nuisances of the West Coast, swaggering, impudent, and generally dishonest and untrustworthy fellows, with Old Testament names and lots of Bible expressions, on every available occasion will bully, as being British subjects. So I thought very likely this fellow was one of them, and properly imprisoned. Immoveable as my audience had remained during the letter part of the business visit, there were distinct signs of general relief when I changed the subject, and we all got pleasant. When I mentioned the name of the prisoner, one Joseph Davies, the King's face beamed with a smile, and his eyes twinkled. I seldom saw a black face that showed so much expression when he smiled and looked pleased. He told me Davies was very troublesome with his tongue, and did much mischief, speaking against him and making disturbances. I said this might be quite true, but that imprisonment should not be so cruel as to endanger health or life, and mentioned the cruelties alleged by Davies. There was a

F

general sort of puff from most of them, as if to say,
"Absurd!" and the King assured me that it was not so.
I then read out an enormous fine that Davies alleged
had been laid upon him, at which the King and all his
people burst out into a roar of laughter, not waiting for
the ceremony of his interpreter re-translating what was
said; and the King quaintly remarked: "If Davies was
taken to the market, and sold there himself, he would
not bring anything like that amount. At the same time,"
he said, "he would release him that day." I offered to
take him off to Lagos, but not if they thought that this
would lead to Davies and his friends boasting that I had
been sent up in the big ship to demand his release.
This made a *great* impression, and I saw that they quite
thought it would have that effect, and greatly appreciated
my not asking for it.

I then told the King that two Lagos traders were said
to have been imprisoned by one of his chiefs. He at
once said that he knew nothing about it, and that no
one had a right to imprison people without his knowing
of it. His dander seemed quite up at the idea of this
encroachment upon his rights, which of course includes
fines; and he promised that he would institute immediate
inquiries, and let me know, if I would wait long enough.
I said I could not wait, but would trust his word.
Somebody then seemed to give him a wrinkle about the
matter, for he added, that he had just heard something
about it, and would make strict inquiries, and let the
Governor know what he had done.

These cases led us into mutual discussions upon an
upright and proper administration of justice; and certainly, much as I tried to bring exalted and proper ideas
upon the subject, I found myself unable to express better
or nobler sentiments than he did. King Solomon and
the Queen of Sheba could not have done better. What
baulked me occasionally was that, during this lighter
portion of the interview, I looked about me, and made
observations, which led me to notice some very bright
and sparkling eyes looking out of a door in the corner
of the court. These I soon saw belonged to a bevy of
very pleasing-looking negro damsels, with a considerable

display of youthful charms, who were evidently trying to get a peep at all that was going on. Twice these eager, merry-looking faces made me lose my cue in the conversation, so that when the interpreter had finished the sentence, I forgot where I had left off; but I soon quickly recovered.

On closing our talk, the King quite burst out, and said we had talked like two brothers, both of the same mind. I cordially agreed with him, and said I hoped we should both prove by our deeds that our words were true.

So ended the palaver, and then sundry bottles of drink were brought in. I was a little anxious about them, and chose, I did not know what, but begged for a small quantity, as I did not drink during the day. I again saluted the King, and found that I had some sort of liquor, hot and strong, and my small quantity was nearly half a tumbler. However, I gulped down a good portion, and chuckled when I saw Mr. Hutchinson had nearly a full tumbler of it. The King then said he did not like me to go away without something, and asked me to accept a *pig*. Now, if the King had offered me one of the damsels that were peeping at us, I should have been severely tried ; but—a pig ! I knew from experience at Accra that the manners and customs of the people enabled the pigs to find their own living as street scavengers, and so I thought what an unlimited amount of free-feeding they must have in Porto Novo. So I thanked the King, and said that my office allowed me to receive no presents, as it might be thought they made me lean to one side more than another, but I thanked him all the same. We then bade good-bye to him and his court, amidst many expressions of hearty satisfaction ; and I felt that the visit was a decided success, which I was glad to find was also the opinion of Mr. Hutchinson and the interpreter, who has had much experience in these interviews.

We then marched back again, making a little detour in the market-place, to look at three heads stuck each upon a pole. One was quite a skull, another getting on in that way, but the third had only been up a few days.

He had committed a murder, for which I should certainly have hanged him ; so I saw nothing to complain of, and think the same mode of procedure might have an excellent effect in some notorious parts of Liverpool and other towns. It kept quite fine during our interview, and we at once got safely on board again, as we could not wait. A merchant came off to the steamer, who fully corroborated the King's account of the Sierra Leone man's imprisonment, as well as my impression of the King himself.

Having got up steam, we fired a parting gun, and at about two o'clock away we went on our return voyage, which was a very pleasant one. We stopped at Badagry, and visited the commandant, a man well on in life, and who has been on the Coast since he was ten years old, and has only been home *once*, &c. He has a black wife, and mulatto results, and is settled for life as an African. We dined on deck, and at about nine o'clock we were safe in the lagoon of Lagos, and arrived in safety at about half-past nine.

This circumstantial account of his visit to the native Prince is not only interesting in itself, as giving a graphic picture of the manners and customs of the people, but also as showing indirectly the genial and sympathetic spirit in which Judge Marshall met the natives with whom he had to do, and his quick appreciation of all that was good in their natural character, as well as his firmness in opposing their revolting cruelties.

We have already shown the affectionate terms on which he lived with the French Fathers at Lagos, and the same geniality which had won the hearts of the boys at the Oratory School at Edgbaston, won for him also the hearts of their little negro brothers in Africa. We may gather this from the following passage in a letter to his mother, dated January 10, 1876:

I had arranged a picnic for our serving-boys. . . . It was a damper to our picnic Captain Graves not going with us, and he had to take a boy who is a general favourite, and who was wild with joy at the prospect of going. But a young German came with us, and the whole establishment went off to a country house, some in boats and some on foot, where the cook gave us as good a breakfast as he ever did here, and "plenty chop" for the boys; and as my stores have come, there was an excellent plum-pudding, and the boys were all wild with joy and amusement. We had races and games, which they entered into with great glee. The German and I took hammocks, which were slung under shady trees, in which we passed the hot hours reading newspapers and sleeping. Mine is one I bought with Hennie in Edinburgh, and is of great use to me.

The same letter contains an account of a Mahommedan festival, and will explain the dread that he had of the spread of Islam in Africa.

Saturday was the great feast of the Mahommedans. I went amongst others to see them assemble for the religious part of it. It was a wonderful sight, and proved more than ever that, however powerless Christianity may be in Africa, this religion is not only making immense strides, but civilizes and raises the negro into quite a superior being. The Sierra Leone niggers infest Lagos, and are a set of lying, thieving, and atrociously impudent fellows. They have been utterly spoilt by Exeter Hall and religious cant, and are a parody both upon civilization and Christianity. When a man does not touch his hat to me, I always know he is a Sierra Leone "gentleman." The Brazilian nigger is a far superior being, quiet, industrious, and respectful; and the native pure and uncivilized, though hideously ugly, is certainly far more industrious than his Gold Coast relations. But all the different sorts of people supply the Mahommedans, and wear the burnous, a flowing robe something like an Anglican surplice, loose trousers, and a turban. And they and the pure natives are trusted in business far

sooner than a Christian.   It is very saddening and
perplexing, too, but facts must be faced.

It was a pretty sight to see them gathering, all in new
clothes, except the pilgrims from the interior, who were
almost in rags, but were especially devout.   Swells came
on horseback, the horse covered with trappings, and
surrounded by attendants with tom-toms, swords, &c.
Many wore embroidered robes from the Niger, others
had them made of bright velvet from Europe.   About
the most conspicuous was a large trader.   His dress
was alternate stripes of green and crimson velvet, and
he drove up in a very prettily turned-out gig, with a
small urchin holding his umbrella as gay as himself.
When the high priest, called the Mahmoud, arrived,
there must have been some five thousand men—no
women—all sitting faced in one direction, which I believe
was towards Mecca.   He got on the top of an earthern
mound, and said some words about Allah, and the vast
assemblage made some response, and finally, all prostrated themselves with their faces and foreheads in the
dust.   They were so close together, and so uniform in
their movements, that it looked like a vast carpet of
patchwork.   The Mahmoud afterwards read passages
out of the Koran, and seemed to preach and offer
prayers.   Then a large Niger sheep was brought to the
mound, and he plunged a great sword-knife into the
animal, which was skinned and cut up in a jiffey.   The
knife was held up in all directions, and whoever looked
on the blood was all right.   This was the finale, and
I then went up to the Mahmoud, and was most affectionately received.   One very pretty feature of the assembly
was the little boy attendants, in dresses as gay as their
masters', carrying mats of skin and straw-work, swords,
&c., for them, and then gathering in picturesque groups
outside the crowd of men.   I should like to have one
for a page.

There was some likelihood of the British Government bringing strong pressure to bear upon the
King of Dahomey, but the expedition to Ashanti
had cost much both in money and in still more

precious lives, and things were allowed to take their course. Mr. Marshall writes:

Lagos, May 18th, 1876.—Our thoughts are now turned towards Dahomey, and I have been doing all I possibly can to precipitate a war with it, in order to break down one of the most accursed Satanic powers existing even in Africa. A fine has been laid upon the King of Dahomey by Commodore Hewitt, and if it is not paid by the 1st of June, operations are to commence by a blockade of the Dahomey coast and ports. What we dread is, lest the home authorities discourage strong measures. They are wanted, for humanity's sake as well as for civilization. Until I know what is going to be done, I cannot form my plans as to leave of absence. My time is up on the 2nd of July, but if there is to be an expedition, I shall certainly volunteer for it, to go with native forces, as I did in the Ashanti War. I look upon it as a direct war upon Satan and all the powers of evil that prevail so terribly in this unfortunate land.

If there is to be no expedition, or if there is no place for me in it, I shall probably go home in August, which, as you may suppose, will be a great delight. I have kept my health very fairly well here, having had but few and slight attacks of fever, and, unless something goes wrong, I shall leave Africa as well as on the day I landed. Altogether, I have much to be thankful for.

He did come home, but a great sorrow awaited him in the death of his dearly-loved mother. It was a consolation to her to see him once more, and his affectionate sympathy helped to soften the blow to his sisters and brothers. His stay in England was but short; for Lord Carnarvon, then Secretary for the Colonies, wished him to return to Lagos with the appointment as senior puisne Judge, but promised him a special leave in the following year, when the new judicial organization had been fairly established on the West Coast. The effect of the climate on the soldiers during the Ashanti War had brought home to the authorities how necessary it was to do everything to save the health of Englishmen employed there ; and it was partly through Mr. Marshall's representations that Lord Carnarvon made the wise regulation that European officials were to have six months' leave after twelve months' service. In April, 1877, the new judges were regularly established with Sir David Chalmers as Chief Justice at Cape Coast, and in August the subject of our memoir was able to be again in England.

The visit was an eventful one for him. Before he had ever dreamed of going to Africa, some five years ago, he had been engaged to Miss Alice Young, youngest daughter of the late C. G. Young, Esq., of Corby, Lincolnshire ; but the engagement had been broken off, as it seemed hopeless for him to provide a suitable home for his bride. Now that he had a good income, and was able to spend six months out of every eighteen in England, he ventured to try his fortune again. He was accepted, but the young lady would not hear of being left in England, and insisted on sharing with her husband the dangers of the climate of the West Coast. Their marriage was blessed, on the 25th of October, by his old friend the Rev. Walter J. B. Richards, D.D., at St. Mary's, Bayswater. He thus speaks of it to Father Livius :

It is, I know well, an excellent thing for me to get married ; and this is, as you know, an old and well-tried attachment, and admits me as a member of the old Catholic families of Lincolnshire, Youngs and Colling-

woods, so that I am not so solitary in the Church as I
was. I was uncommonly pleased that circumstances took
us to St. Mary's to get married, and Richards was equally
pleased to tie the knot.

Do not suppose that I am ashamed of my Brother
Bernard days. I had a happy and a useful home among
the Oblates, and the friendships then formed still remain.
Our paths have certainly been different; and I am
thankful to think, that I too am, I hope, of some use
now, both in my professional position and as a friend
to the Catholic missionaries. What grieves me about
them is, that the missionary zeal of English Catholics
should be all expended on the United States, instead of
on English colonies.

The marriage proved a very happy one. Four
years afterwards, he thus wrote to a friend :

I met her through being secretary at a bazaar for
industrial schools and a Convent of the Good Shepherd,
and though it then seemed sheer madness, I got engaged
to her. The Mother Superior of the convent told me
she had prayed that I might be rewarded for my trouble
by getting a good *wife.* We were separated by my
misfortunes, as I thought, finally; until, on my second
visit home, I seemed *forced* and compelled to go and
see her; which I did, and in five minutes was done for;
and mercifully for me, she was not averse. And now,
the longer we live together, the more complete is our
love, and the deeper the love, the more convinced I am
it is a love blessed by God, and a heavenly blessing to
me.

They sailed for their West African home on
January 5, 1878, and were hospitably entertained
by Sir Samuel Rowe at Sierra Leone, and exactly
a month after they had started from Liverpool
they anchored in Lagos Roads.

Next morning the Government steamer, *Nelly,* came
out to take us on shore, and I felt proud and gratified at

the reception given to my brave wife. According to ordinary rule, Governors receive only in Government House, sending an aide-de-camp or other official to meet distinguished guests. With this official it is a further matter of consideration and etiquette whether he remains on the wharf to receive the guest there, or goes on board to welcome him. On this occasion, I saw a crowd on the wharf, and the first to come on board was the Governor, Mr. Dumaresq, with a hearty welcome to my wife, followed by the chief officials and many leading merchants, both native and European, all anxious to give a real good welcome to the white lady, who had left her home in England to come out with "the Judge" to a country sometimes called "the white man's grave." Among these I need scarcely add, I soon saw the white serge robes of the Padres, whose welcomes were doubtless the deepest and sincerest of all.[1]

The fears which Mr. Marshall had not unreasonably felt as to the effect of the climate on his wife were happily not justified by the result. She was always well on the West Coast; and, though in this very year, 1878, his own health began to give way, it was mainly through his wife's nursing that he was able to serve out his time. Lagos, situated on a flat sandy island, full of swamps, with a population of forty thousand inhabitants, is one of the most unhealthy places of the West Coast. Moreover, every now and then it is visited by a fever somewhat resembling the yellow fever of the West Indies.

In the May of 1878, one of these epidemics swept over Lagos, and one of the earliest victims was a bright young Irish Sister, the first who had come from Ireland. She died on the 7th of May, and was buried the same evening. On the following Sunday, a young priest, Père Poussin, followed her to the grave. He had only

[1] *Reminiscences,* p. 38.

been out a short time, and was but twenty-three years of age. He had been a great favourite at the Novitiate, and was full of life and spirit. On the Saturday evening he had a slight fever, his first, and he took it quite merrily. The next morning, Père Baudin, who sang the High Mass at nine, left him in good spirits. When we came out of the chapel I was told he was dying. I hastened to the mission-house, but before I got there I heard the tolling of the passing-bell, and found him insensible and dying, surrounded by all his brethren, and in a short time he was dead. He was buried the same day, the Governor and suite attending. I then began to feel ill myself, and on the following Thursday I was in a hard swim for life. For three days and nights I struggled between life and death, and was only saved by the tender nursing of my wife, ably assisted by a colonial surgeon, Dr. M'Carthy. On the Monday evening a steamer homeward bound arrived, and I was ordered off at once in her.[1]

During this stay in England, on the 10th of November, their firstborn, James Bernard, was born ; and, as soon as the child could be safely left in charge of their relatives, his parents returned to Lagos, the frost of an English winter having quite restored the Judge's health. In 1879, Sir David Chalmers was promoted to Guiana, and Mr. Marshall received instructions to proceed to Accra, and take up the duties of the Chief Justice, although he was not gazetted until the following year. He gives a graphic description of their difficulties in leaving Lagos, owing to the surf on the bar.

We were in the small Government steamer which was to take us over the bar and out to the steamer bound for Accra. We knew the bar was bad that day, and could see the line of white curling breakers that broke over it,

---

[1] *Reminiscences*, p. 40.

but it was not supposed that there would be any difficulty or danger in crossing it in a steamboat. In case of her shipping heavy seas we took up our position on the bridge beside the captain, and so we saw everything. As we approached the line of breakers I saw how terrible they were, rearing straight up, and then curling over in a deep mass of beautiful green, which broke in huge torrents of foam. But the captain did not seem to fear any danger, and we went steadily on right into the midst of them. To my horror I perceived that soon the steamer made no way. Wave after wave broke over the bows in rapid succession, sending volumes of water along the deck, which poured down into the engine-rooms. Presently the ventilators were swept away, leaving apertures down which the water poured more rapidly than ever. I could no longer say a word to assure my wife that there was no danger, nor could any one else. I saw safety a few yards behind and a few yards in front, but there we lay helpless, battered by these huge breakers, and lying in the very middle of the cruel seething waters, which I feared in a few minutes would be our graves. Had I been alone, perhaps I could have felt more resigned; but the wife, who had come out a second time with me, was by my side, and our little infant boy was at home. I could only think how *cruel* it all looked. But I heard her prayers, and I saw also James Gordon[1] come and kneel on the paddle-box close beside us and pray most earnestly, and I tried to hope. Presently the paddle-wheels stopped altogether, so I knew the engine had ceased to work, and that as soon as the vessel got broadside to the waves, we should go down among the sharks which swarm about there. Humanly speaking, we were saved by having an English engineer on board, who set to work himself and made the men work with a will. I remember that he made three men hang on to a valve which had got broken or put out of order, and he himself

---

[1] A little Fanti boy, rescued during the war by Colonel Gordon, and afterwards instructed and baptized by the Fathers, Mr. and Mrs. Marshall being his sponsors. An account is given of him in the *Reminiscences*, pp. 41—48, which illustrates the difficulty of fixing Christian ideas in the minds of these natives. In this case the conversion, though sorely tried, proved genuine.

gave a comical touch to the tragic scene by placing his burly person on one of the holes left by the carrying away of a ventilator, where he held on amidst the seas that rushed upon him. Presently the engines moved, and the engineer, getting up, said to the captain, "For God's sake go astern." The word was given, the wheels revolved, and in another minute we were safe, and went back to Lagos.[1]

In July, 1880, they both returned to England, and purchased a small villa at St. Marychurch, near Torquay, where it was intended that Mrs. Marshall should remain with their little boy and a baby girl, Alice Mary, who was born there on the 23rd of November. Mr. Marshall had a wonderful power of recovering his health. Sometimes he would be hurried on board a home-bound ship in the lowest stage of illness, and during the voyage would pick up his strength to such an extent that he felt quite ashamed of presenting himself at the Colonial Office as an invalid. By the end of 1880 he considered himself quite well enough to go out alone, though his affectionate disposition caused him to feel loneliness very keenly, after the comfort of more than three years of married life. He tried to console himself by writing for his wife a full diary of all that took place from his parting with her at Plymouth to go on board the *Nubia*.

My Alice, how am I to live without you? But that "won't do." . . . I am glad your loneliness is not like mine. . . . The saloon is an immense comfort, and I sat there till near ten, when I crept off to my cabin, and there tried to pray, and did pray for my dear ones, and wished I could cry—I felt it would relieve me—but could not. I got out my rug, and put it over the bunk

[1] *Reminiscences*, pp. 43, 44.

which would have been yours, if you had been with me.
I said my Rosary, with my usual Joyful Mysteries inten-
tions, and thankfully fell asleep. . . . Dear Allie, what
a pain there is in love like ours, when fate separates us !
But it is God, not fate, and may He bless it to us both,
and to our little ones.

Jan. 20th. Bay of Biscay.—I wish you knew what a
lovely morning this is here. . . . I wish I could feel
more bright myself, but my aching heart feels some
comfort in sitting down to write to you, my precious
one.   When at last we prepared to start, I am glad to
say all the selfish sorrow I felt at having let you go away
was swallowed up and lost in thankfulness that I did
persuade you to go. . . . I keep my watch at your
time, so as to say my morning prayers at eight with you,
and to think of what you are doing.

21*st.*—I am glad to think that by this time you will
have written to me, and that to-morrow your letter will
be on its way.   Be sure to try and say your morning
prayers about eight, for it is an immense comfort to me
to think we are joining in prayer at the same time ; and
I will also continue to think of you at the week-day
Benedictions, and will try and say my Rosary on those
days at 4.30.

Saturday, 22*nd.*—I have just been saying Rosary and
Benediction with you on deck at your time of 4.30 ; and
will always try and do so, walking up and down the deck
on the side associated with you. . . . I suppose in time
my poor aching heart will get less sensitive to its pain,
and I shall become more reconciled to my lonely fate,
but it is not so yet. . . . At eight, by English time,
I say "our" prayers.   Be sure and keep regular at
Benediction, and be *in time* for the Rosary.   I cannot
tell you what a comfort it is to me when I can picture
you in church, occupying my place, so that I can join
with you in spirit and in heart.

Sunday, Jan. 23*rd.*—This has been a *very* hard
morning, for it has opened all my wounds afresh.   At
eight by English time, though it was seven here, I tried
to say Mass and pray with you, but it was heart-breaking,
and when I came to the *Memento*, and begged for my

wife and children, at last I sobbed, and found relief in tears. I sat on my portmanteau beside the bunk, but it looked so empty without you, that I was glad to kneel on the ground, leaning on the seat, but could find neither comfort nor devotion—it seemed all so hard and bitter. God forgive me for saying so, and enable me to be more resigned! I am thankful you have that darling boy and your wee baby to comfort, amuse, and occupy you. . . . Kiss Bernard for "poor pap-pa on the wa-tah." I love to think of his little prayer for me, and may God in His mercy help me through this time of suffering and trial. My darling wife, no words can tell you how bitterly I feel this separation from you whom I love so dearly, and who have been so loving and kind to me. . . . I fear I have grumbled too much in this letter, but it relieves me to tell you everything, and I suppose in time my heart-aches will get deadened.

Jan. 24th.—We are in sight of Teneriffe, on a lovely morning, and I was on deck, pacing up and down, thinking of you, when old Digges (the captain) came to me, and said we should meet the *Majemba* at Teneriffe, sɔ that I could send you another letter, and that if I did not he would tell you that I did not consider you worth 2½d., the postage. So here I am writing again, and suppose it will reach you with the letter I left for you at Madeira. . . . However, I am glad to think that my telegram yesterday would put your mind at ease. . . . I am very glad I am sailing with old Digges, if it is only on account of his "family" feelings. He takes great care of me. The first evening at sea he found me out on the deck in the bitter cold, and bundled me in, saying he had charge of me now you were not with me, so I was to "turn in." I cannot tell you what a comfort it is to me to get these little pieces of sympathy from him, especially as he knows you.

After writing this morning I joined the doctor and purser, who were talking about the Catholic religion, and the purser claimed me as one of the household of faith. I had been reading the *Tablet*, and left it on my seat, and it was seen by him and the doctor. I rather thought the purser was a Catholic, as I was sure the Bath Canon

whom I met at Brownlow's asked me if I had met
Dennis, which is his name. I then found it was so.
But the queer part was, the doctor asked me if I was
not the son of Mr. Marshall, the Scotch clergyman of
Glasgow and Edinburgh, whose sister, Miss Marshall,
lived in Edinburgh. He even mentioned to me the
street in Edinburgh in which I was born, and then told
me that his father knew mine well, and he himself knew
my dear old aunt, and a deal about me and all of us.
I fear he must also know that I was a parson, but, if so,
I hope he will keep quiet about it.

Jan. 27th.—Early yesterday morning we were off
Grand Canary, and for the first time I went on deck in
pyjamas, and found it too cold. I came in for a lovely
sight, the rising sun lighting up the Canary hills, and
also the Peak of Teneriffe above a mass of clouds. It
was only for a few minutes, as the clouds soon rose with
a mist, and also, as we rounded the island, Teneriffe was
hidden from us.

As we were to be at Canary for some hours, and I had
never been on shore there, I went on shore after breakfast. . . . The sea was calm, and it was excessively hot
on shore. I still wore my thick suit, and had no
umbrella, so I was not sorry when we got to the agent's
place. I had no wish to go with the doctor and the
negro passenger, especially to the Cathedral, as I have a
great dislike to going into our churches with Protestants,
and I wanted to go *alone*. So I gave them the slip, and
soon found a church, which was a refuge from the heat
and glare of the sun, and also for my aching heart.
I never felt more thankful that I belonged to the
Catholic Church, in which one is at home in all lands
and among all nations, nor more thankful for the abiding
Presence in the Blessed Sacrament. And as I knelt in
the silent and empty church, alone, and yet so near our
Lord, and poured out my prayers to Him and His dear
Mother, I felt a comfort and relief that I have not known
since I parted from you. I begged for blessings on you
and my Bernard and "baybee," and for grace to bear my
trial, and then went on to the Cathedral. It is well worth
a visit, but I was glad that I had had my pray in a quieter

church. The pillars are like very tall palm-trees, and the choir is in the centre of the nave, like in some old Basilica churches at Rome. The vestments and plate are, I believe, magnificent, but I did not see them. If ever you are out in these parts again I must try and take you to see this very fine and curious church. I then strolled back to the quay.

As time passed, he seemed more able to enjoy things around him, and to find an interest in his books, though the home-sickness still clung to him. He often speaks of the kind sympathy of the captain.

Monday, 31st.—Yesterday finished with a glorious afternoon, which I thought even you must have admired. A cool breeze sprang up, and we glided quietly through the calm sea, looking at many an ugly fin of sharks, with occasional sun-fish, and finishing by getting into the middle of an immense shoal of porpoises, rolling and jumping all round us. . . . I am more and more interested in Green's *History (of the English People)*, and his hearty sympathy with the struggles of the people against the tyranny of kings, barons, lordly bishops, and wealthy burghers delights me, especially as he has very considerable appreciation for the noble part the English monks and priests, with many a noble prelate, bore in it. Old Digges is so struck with my interest in it, that he has written to his wife to buy it for him.

Some rather startling intelligence reached him at Sierra Leone.

Government House, Sierra Leone, Feb. 2nd.—We arrived here about 3.30, and you may imagine my feelings when the pilot came on board, and told us that the Ashantis had broken out in war against us again, and that a lot of the West Indian Regiment had gone down to Cape Coast. As soon as Streeten heard I was on board he came off for me, and confirmed the news so far, that

G

Mr. Griffiths, our acting Governor, had written off here for troops, on account of an expected Ashanti invasion, and had paid the captain of the *Corisco* £1,000 to come straight to Sierra Leone with his letter. He has also asked that all ships of war may be sent there. . . . Griffiths may have taken unnecessary fright. Don't you disturb yourself unnecessarily about it, and wait patiently for further accounts. Even if it is true, I can hardly imagine that the Ashantis would invade, with the rainy season coming on so soon. It is quite pleasant to have an excitement like this to occupy my thoughts, and I am writing to the *Manchester Guardian* to say that I shall recommence writing to them, if there is anything to write about.

It proved to be a mere scare, as Marshall found when he got to Lagos. We know not whether our readers will care to read any more extracts from those loving letters, written in the sweet confidence of conjugal affection. But in days when people are asking : " Is Marriage a Failure ? " it is refreshing to meet with unmistakeable proofs of the reality and strength of true wedded love. A picture of James Marshall would not be complete without a glance into this tender side of his character, which was as fresh in him at fifty as it is in youthful lovers at twenty. What is still more worthy of notice is that, strong and even passionate as this affection was, it was always permeated through and through with the love of God, and was in loyal subordination to the will of God. It was sanctified by prayer, and cemented by the grace of the sacraments, and hence, though it might be the occasion of acute pain, yet it never left any remorse behind. Perhaps another extract or two may be permitted.

I have much to learn yet, which I am certain God alone can teach me. Before I left you, and especially when in church, I felt full of good resolutions and bravery, and quite resolved to love the cross that I had to bear. But that is all gone now, and I fear I anything but love it. I do thank God that you have that darling boy with you, and "baybee" to occupy your time, attention, and love. And perhaps when I hear from you I shall get happier and more resigned. I thank God that the keen mental suffering I have endured since I left you has not injured me in health, which makes me confident that God is helping me. . . I picked a leaf off an orange at Canary, which I intend to send to you, and foolish-like I have kissed it again and again, because it is going to you, and because I know that you will kiss it too. Things like this may be romantic folly between lovers, but they are a comforting reality to me in my love for you, my precious wife, when away from me.

I have just been comforting myself by saying the Rosary, with Benediction, singing quietly the *Magnificat*, as it is Saturday, beginning a few minutes after 4.30 by your time, as I know the Canon is apt to be a little late on Saturdays.

Sunday, 30th.—I said the Mass at eight this morning, and got through it better than last Sunday. The Collect for the Sunday, Fourth after Epiphany, suited me very well, and the Gospel, our Lord bringing a calm on the stormy sea, seemed to calm my poor troubled heart a little. But it is all so different, and I felt glad when I had finished. I fear this is but a selfish letter, but be assured, though I pour out my troubles to you, that I will try and be brave, and put into practice the good resolutions we made. I trust you to keep bright and happy in the little home I was so glad and proud to make for you, with your two bairns beside you. . . . I have been lying down in the deck-house, and my thoughts have been busy on how much I owe to that love; and I have a happy confidence that God will spare me to live in that love again, deepened and blessed by this sore trial. If it should be otherwise, I must leave little Bernard to take my place, and endeavour still to say, *Fiat voluntas*

tua. . . . I have been putting some additional kisses
on the orange-leaf for Bernard, for I want you to ask him
to kiss it too, and tell him it comes from " Pap-pa in the
boat on the wa-tah."

He landed at Accra; but in March his duties led
him to Elmina, where he had the consolation of
seeing Père Moreau and another Father beginning
their work there. In April, as Chief Justice, he
went to Lagos,where he and the two puisne Judges
had some cases of appeal to decide. He was glad
of the opportunity of spending Easter with the
missionaries. He writes an account to his wife.

Lagos, Easter Sunday, April 17th, 1881.—I have been
to Mass this morning, and offered my Communion for
you, and have prayed that yours for me might be blessed
to me, for I know that I have by far the best of the
exchange. . . . I felt too tired to go to the High Mass,
and so am quiet here. You know how trying the chapel
here is at all times, but especially on crowded days. . . .
There were considerably more communicants than I have
ever seen before, and Père Chausse seems to think they
have a little more consolation in Lagos. . . . Dr. M'Carthy
continues very kind and attentive to the mission, without
any pay. He is a nice fellow. I was the only white
male communicant, so I supposed they have not improved
in that way.

April 18th.—I went to breakfast with the Padres
yesterday, who seemed highly pleased with my company.
I was the only guest. We talked a great deal, and after
the eating part, they drank to the health of Madame
Marshall, and the little boy and the little girl, with much
animation, pleasing me greatly. They told me that there
had been a large number of male communicants at the
chapel there as well as at the High Mass at the church,
and altogether the mission seems to have made great
progress, and to be in a very hopeful state. Père
Chausse thinks they will be in the new church at

Whitsuntide. . . . I went to the Benediction, when the church looked very bright and pretty, with the gay colours and dresses of the women and girls. The singing has made great advance, as they have a good musician among the Padres. When the *O salutaris* was sung, my loneliness came heavily home to me, and I had to shut up my singing. But listening to *Da robur, fer auxilium*, went to my heart, and *Nobis donet in patria* became a prayer for a native home-land with my wife, more than the one meant in the hymn. The reality of the Unity of the Catholic Church and the Blessed Sacrament again came home very forcibly to me, like that day in Grand Canary, and though I felt an exile, yet I also was in sweet union with you, my own true wife.

After Benediction, I went with Père Chausse to see the Sisters—seven of them. The Sister Superior asked very affectionately after you and the babies. They won't speak English, so I was glad to get away, but they seemed much gratified with the visit. Poor things! I wish they had a larger and more airy house. . . . The visit here has been a very pleasant one, thanks to Moloney's hospitality.

Do you keep up night prayers? If you do, I want you *all* to say an *Our Father* and *Hail Mary* for me in them. Tell the (servant) girls it is at my request, and that I always pray for all my household in my prayers. It is very sweet to think of that dear little boy praying for me.

He started for Accra the day that this letter was finished, and though he took every precaution against the fever, he found himself attacked by it in May. It then became a serious question with his wife, whether she should leave her little ones and go out alone to nurse her sick husband. At length she decided to go, and bravely set out from Plymouth, leaving her children under the care of her kind "Aunt Pollie." After she had sailed, letters brought us better accounts, and we were able to console her at Madeira with the telegram :

" James convalescent." The following extracts from letters written during this time will show how severely his spirits were tried, and also how strong was that faith which supported him through so many trials. He had been reading *The History of St. Catherine of Siena*, by Miss Drane, of Stone. He writes, June 6, 1881 :

I became ill, and have been so more or less for more than five weeks, and my feeling now is, that if she (his wife) does not come, my chances of stopping out my time will be greatly lessened. The heroics are gone, and I do thank the Sisters for their kindness in thinking of me. . . . The Life of St. Catherine of Siena has fascinated me. I never read anything like that before; or is it that sickness and solitude in a sort of hermitage have brought me a little more sense ? It seems to have given me a kind of personal acquaintance with her, so that I have prayed to her for health and help in a way that seems new to me. I am sorry to say that Saints have generally appeared to me from what I have read of them to be disagreeable, severe, and rude to all in the world; but St. Catherine, with all the wonders of her sanctity, must have been on earth something marvellously loveable and attractive. Ever since I left England, I have united my Mass-prayers with your eight o'clock Mass, and generally the week-day Rosary and Benediction. Now that I know of St. Catherine, and that the Mother Prioress (Mother Rose Columba, now in Adelaide) and the Sisters are *hers*, I am more drawn to this than ever, and do beg for their kind prayers to St. Catherine for me and mine. I have been very unwell, and very unhappy, with a great fear lest I was to be taken away, out here in exile from home and Church ; but perhaps it will prove good for me, removing a few more excrescences. Imagine me, of all people, left for five weeks, in a house by myself, ill and down-hearted, with only one real friend in the place, whom I only saw very occasionally, having to occupy myself as best I could. Yet I cannot bear to be taken away from here. For a few days, ill as I was, I had to go to Elmina, but I was thankful to get back to my lonely life, and I limit my reading of St. Catherine, so as to make it last longer. I fear I am indulging in self-conceit again, in writing this to you; but I write it to you, if I may say so, spiritually, as I should be glad that you should know that being ground in the mill may prove God's goodness to me, in at last making me learn something. I hope you will all pray much for my brave wife. None of you can realize what the voyage will be to her all alone. . . . I am glad the bairns have been consecrated to our Blessed Lady, and so placed under her special protection. . . . I often wish I could make as full a confession to a priest as I sometimes can here all alone, and without so many distractions. I wear what is left of the scapular, and hope Alice will bring me a new one.

June 8th.—I was much better when I began this letter, but grieve to say I have had another severe return. It is a sore time of trial to me, and the dread of what may happen weighs at times heavily upon me. . . . I have begun a novena to St. Catherine for my health to-day. I feel I may ask for it on behalf of my wife and little ones. . . . I got to my Easter duties at Lagos, and was so pleased to see that the mission is really beginning to show power.

June 16th.—This is Corpus Christi, and in my exile my heart is with you all. It is also the ninth day of my novena to St. Catherine of Siena, and I feel constrained to write again to you to tell you that this last day has been a thanksgiving from my grateful heart for a recovery from my long and obstinate illness. I am not telling, still less I trust boasting, of anything supernatural. I have told you of the way St. Catherine's Life laid hold of me, both in my heart and my intellect, arousing, I trust, a little of what is due to God in the one, and a beginning of true sense or knowledge in the other. Her kind thoughtful love for her friends, kindest to those who, like Stephen Maconi, needed it most, drew me to her at a time when I was in great distress and anxiety about my health, and then it flashed upon me to offer a novena.

I began it on the 8th, and asked her to pray for my
restoration to health, by obtaining a blessing on the
means used. The 6th and 7th were very bad days with
me, and I greatly feared what might be in store for me,
for remember this was the sixth week of this constant
irritation of the bowels day and night. I tell you the
plain truth when I say, that from my first day's offering
to St. Catherine on the morning of the 8th, I have
steadily improved, and to-day look upon myself as *well*,
although, of course I shall have to be very careful for a
few days more. I hope I am not presumptuous in writing
this to you. I do so because of the special and peculiar
union that binds me to you, and now also to your church
and the convent, because of the kind and useful friend,
if I may venture to use the word, I have found in their
wonderful St. Catherine. I shall be so grateful if you
can in some way offer a thanksgiving to St. Catherine
for me, if only a word at the altar, and perhaps Mother
Prioress will also do so for me.

In January, 1882, Chief Justice Marshall was
ordered home by the medical authorities, as the
only hope of saving his life ; and he was ill for
some time after his return. On the 29th of June,
by Her Majesty's command, he went down to
Windsor, and received the honour of knighthood
at the hands of the Queen. He wished very much
to have been able to go out again to his post on
the Gold Coast, but the medical authorities at the
Colonial Office said it would never do ; so, on the
15th of July he resigned, greatly to the regret of
all who had known him in the colony.

CHAPTER V.

LIFE IN ENGLAND. ROYAL NIGER COMPANY.
INDIAN AND COLONIAL EXHIBITION. EXPE-
DITION TO THE NIGER. WEST AFRICAN
MISSIONS.

SIR JAMES MARSHALL was now settled for life
in England; but his active disposition made it
impossible for him to remain idle. At the request
of Lord Aberdare, he accepted a place on the
directorate of the National African Company, and
his knowledge of the West Coast enabled him to
render valuable service at the meetings of the
Board, which he regularly attended. This neces-
sitated his leaving St. Marychurch, and he took
a house at Roehampton, close to the grounds of
Manresa. Here he was always on the most
intimate terms of friendship with the Jesuit
Fathers; had the benefit of their prayers and
advice in many a difficulty; and, by his example
and zeal in every good work, proved himself a
valuable friend to the little mission of Roehampton. He threw himself heartily into every movement which seemed likely to promote the cause
of religion; and when, through the exertions of
his old friend the Bishop of Salford, Father Clarke,
S.J., Father Cologan, and Mr. James Britten, the

Catholic Truth Society, which had remained in a state of suspended animation for some years, was revived into vigorous activity, Sir James became an active member of the committee, and subsequently treasurer, and, by his energy and knowledge of business, contributed not a little to its success.

But he never forgot the West Coast of Africa. Whatever else engaged his attention and his sympathies, the needs of the poor people among whom he had lived so long, and especially the needs of the struggling Catholic missions there were always very near to his heart. He kept up a regular correspondence with the Fathers at Lagos and Elmina, and did all that he could to call attention to the wants of their missions by writing to the *Tablet*, and procuring the insertion in that paper of several interesting letters from Père Moreau, describing his visit to Coomassie and the King of Ashanti. We should have liked to have inserted these letters, but we must confine ourselves to the subject of this memoir. He wrote:

August 21*st*, 1882.—My own personal connection with the Gold Coast is, I am sorry to say, at an end; but I shall be glad to be allowed to make one more appeal on behalf of this most strangely neglected part of Africa, where I well know the Church is losing splendid opportunities of establishing missions which could penetrate far into the interior, as fast as men and money could be provided.

He mentions the establishment of the Apostolic College at Cork, and expresses his hope that Père Moreau's appeal for aid will not be left unanswered.

If not, if no help in a substantial form is given to him and his mission, it can but dwindle on from hand to mouth in Elmina; his strength, health, and spirits will succumb to the climate, whilst the Protestant missions, which are at present quite staggered by his success, will go smilingly on, making themselves comfortable and secure throughout the country.

This opinion is confirmed by a letter from Père Moreau, published in the *Tablet* of October 7th:

We are not progressing much, but we are not losing ground. A Wesleyan minister has been removed to a small village, because he did not resist effectually enough the "encroachments of Roman Catholicism." His successor is showing more zeal. He has been doing his best to annihilate our school, but it was more than he could do. On Sundays, he never misses to say something against us, but the things most absurd and calumnious. . . . The result is the opposite he intended. . . . People say to themselves, "It cannot be so; let us go and ask the Father;" and many have come to me for this reason.

In 1884 the Berlin Conference awakened the attention of Englishmen to the importance of our West African possessions, and Sir James Marshall considered it a fitting opportunity for him to put before English Catholics the necessity for doing something more for the missions on that coast. Accordingly he published in the *Tablet* the following paper on

WEST AFRICAN MISSIONS AND THE BERLIN CONFERENCE.

During the last ten years I have at various times endeavoured, by means of the Catholic Press, to draw attention to the great and increasing importance of the missions in West Africa. My long residence on the

Gold Coast made me feel sure that the best entrance into the heart of Africa, both for missionary and commercial enterprise, was from the West Coast, if only on account of the great river that enters the sea on its long line. Whilst large sums of money, as well as many precious lives, were being spent, and to a great extent lost, on missions in North and Central Africa, I tried all I could to plead for the missionary efforts of Catholic England and the Propaganda to be directed to West Africa, where there was the protection of the British Government, as well as native populations well-disposed towards missionaries, with, at the same time, a safer and better basis for operation in the interior than would be got anywhere else.

For reasons I have never been able to understand, the West African Missions have been kept on the smallest scale possible, with a constant cutting down of the allowances made. And now the scramble for Africa among European nations has come, and I hope the Propaganda, like our Foreign Office, is being awakened to the fact that West Africa is the principal scene of the scramble. Until a short time ago, Great Britain might have secured any part of the West Coast she pleased. The mouths of the Niger, the Cameroons, the line of coast that now intervenes between the Gold Coast and its largest town of Lagos, the Congo—all these and other parts were within her reach, and many of them were pressed upon her. Now Germany has crept in upon and occupied one portion of the Gold Coast line; France another. Germany has also taken the Cameroons, and the Congo is being arranged for. The opportunity is gone, and all Great Britain can hope for is to be able to hold on to the Niger country, thanks to the hold which her merchants have got upon it. In a similar way the West Coast of Africa has been at the disposal of the Propaganda for missions. Our Government welcomes, supports, and protects missions, the Catholic as much as the others. The natives also welcome the white missionaries who seek to do good, though they are sharp in distinguishing the real missionary from the make up which is often found among them. Had the West Coast been occupied by Catholic missions to any such extent as has been attempted in the north, and on the Zambesi River and other parts of the interior, with terrible disasters and at enormous expense, yet without much success, the Church would have been more ready to follow in the opening-up of Africa which is now taking place from the West.

At Lagos, the French Society of African Missions has done a great work under immense disadvantages, especially under that most disastrous economy in keeping it poor, and without anything like sufficient means, while thousands of pounds went where comparatively nothing could be done. Notwithstanding this, the progress there has been wonderful. When I first went to Lagos in 1874, a mere handful went to Mass, and I scarcely ever saw a man at Holy Communion. I wish now to publish, as widely as I can, some extracts from a letter I have just received from Père Chausse, the Superior of Lagos, telling of their present position.

" Our missions are getting on well, and are developing under the blessing of God. In 1873, there were three adults who performed their Easter duties. Last Easter we had nearly nine hundred communicants. The Mass is well attended. Christian marriages are held in honour, and the schools have given great satisfaction to the Government inspector. We have four hundred scholars, whose studies are conducted in English. But the missionaries learn to make use of the native language. Catechism, instructions, and confessions are all conducted in ' Nago,' to the great profit of souls. Père Baudin, who has been for a year at Lyons, has printed a Catechism in the native language, as well as a French-Zorouba and Zorouba-French Dictionary. On the 8th of December we shall have nearly ninety children who will, on that day, make their First Communion here at Lagos. On that day also, in accordance with the powers given me by the Holy See, I shall administer to them the Sacrament of Confirmation. On All Saints' Day I shall be at Porto Novo for that purpose, and, in January, at Abeokuta, a very large town in the interior. This last station prospers, and I have found it necessary to send a third missionary to meet its wants. At Lagos, if it were not that we have not got the necessary funds, we could open several more schools, and have hundreds more scholars from among the children, who, from not being under the influence of the missionaries, are being lost. Would that the charitable souls of England and Ireland would come to our assistance in this colony which belongs to them. During this year death has removed two of the missionaries who have been longest with us, Pères André and Durien. They had been home to France, to recruit and take a little rest. They were both at out-stations, and came here for medical aid against dysentery, and they died in the midst of us. It is a heavy loss to our missions. Pray for them. The Propaganda having detached Dahomey and the countries as far as the Volta from the vicariate of Benin, has erected a separate vicariate of Dahomey. It has also founded the prefecture of the Niger, and confided it also to our Society. The first missionaries are now on their way to the Niger."

This is wonderful progress, and there would be far greater if men and money were provided more liberally for these missions, to enable the missionaries to meet a tithe of the wants of the countries they are sent to. There is not a single Bishop on the whole coast from Sierra Leone to Gaboon. All their appeals are met with the response that there are not sufficient funds, and repeatedly they have been told that they must do with less, as the French Catholics could not, or did not, subscribe as much as they did formerly, and they gave less to these missions in particular, as they belonged to an English colony, and ought to be supported more by England. There would be nothing to say to this, if it were not for the fact that immense sums—immense at all events in comparison with what has been given to West Africa—have been given to be spent in parts like Egypt and North Africa, where scarcely any converts have been made, except among the negro slaves taken there from the very regions of Africa where this Society labours. Large sums have also gone to missions in the interior, which have produced heartrending tales of suffering, privation, and death, but no record of success like that which follows the West African missionaries wherever they go. I remember reading a report of the journey of the missionaries to the Zambesi station, in which it was stated that each waggon and its bullocks cost £1,000. No such sum ever reaches the West African missionaries, though if it did it would bring in scores of converts.

The opening-up of Africa for trade is going on with a rapidity which astonishes even those who have been engaged in the trade for years. The nations of Europe are dividing the vast continent among themselves, with West Africa as their basis of operations. One English company has pushed its stations on the Niger as far as eight hundred miles from its mouth. The Protestant missions are being extended in all directions. Having resided in West Africa, and among the Catholic missionaries there, I venture to ask the Catholic Press to allow me to set forth the immense importance at this time of these missions. It is these missions which must unite a Catholic invasion of Africa to the invasion of trade and exploration. On the scale on which this is done depends the Catholic future of all that part of the African continent.

A letter from Père Moreau from Elmina, incorporated in this paper, has been omitted for the sake of brevity. The *Tablet* of December 6, 1884, in which this paper was printed, remarks:

The long and varied experience of Sir James Marshall at the Gold Coast, and the distinguished service he has rendered there in more than one capacity, must lend peculiar importance to anything he may have to say about the land he knows so well.

In the following year Sir James sent to the same paper a letter from Père Chausse, in which he gives an account of Father Holley's expedition to Oyo, the capital of the Yoruba country, the

King of which had promised to enclose a piece
of ground for the mission :

> The King has built walls five feet high, which form a
> beautiful enclosure for the splendid piece of ground just
> named, situated at the junction of the three roads that
> divide the capital.   The King would only accept a few
> small presents for this, and wished me to send some
> missionaries as soon as possible, and promised that on
> their arrival he would build them a house under their
> own direction, as well as a chapel and a church. . . .
> May God be praised !   What a splendid field this opens
> for missionaries !   It is the great heathen kingdom which
> rules over great cities like Ibadan, which equals Abeokuta
> in size.   Beg of the Master of the vineyard to send more
> labourers.

Later on in the same year he had to announce
the death of Father Holley, on which occasion the
King of Yoruba sent a special embassy to Lagos,
to express his sorrow and sympathy.

These papers of Sir James Marshall were translated into French and laid before the Council of
Propaganda, but it was not until three years afterwards that they produced any practical effect.   In
October, 1886, he wrote to the *Tablet* to announce
the death of Père Moreau, the Superior at Elmina,
and he says somewhat bitterly :

> Of course his death has been attributed to the fatal
> climate.   Often has he told me and written to me, that
> he and his companions, including some unfortunate
> Sisters, could do but little—in fact, could scarcely keep
> themselves alive, because of the "starvation" allowance
> on which they had to exist.   In writing to tell me of his
> death, Father Michou, his successor, said but too truly
> that he did not die of disease, but of a broken heart,
> worn out by care and disappointment at the neglect and

abandonment of his mission.   The colonial doctor who attended him at the last, though unknown to me, wrote to me as their friend, begging me to try and get these good men saved from inevitable death, not from climate, but from overwork and want of proper nourishment and living.

The Indian and Colonial Exhibition of 1886 afforded Sir James Marshall an opportunity for bringing the West Coast before the notice of Englishmen ; and though its products are not of a very attractive character, as compared with the products of many other parts of the British Empire, he managed to secure for them a considerable space, and stirred up a spirit of emulation at Lagos and other places to do their best.   Sir James was Commissioner for the West Coast, and threw himself heart and soul into the work.   His services were well appreciated by the Prince of Wales, and he received from the Queen, in the August of that year, the Companionship of St. Michael and St. George.

The importance of our African possessions are now more fully understood than was the case four years ago.   Germany and France have awakened us from our apathy, and that which long African experience had taught the subject of this memoir, has been brought home to the nation generally by the inexorable logic of accomplished facts.   The papers contributed to *The Month* in 1886, on the River Niger and its Future, show how thoroughly Sir James Marshall had grasped what our statesmen had been so slow to learn.   In the first paper, he traces the history of our possessions on the West Coast, and especially of the Niger territory.

H

In his second paper he sketches the "Mission Prospects on the Niger," and endeavours to arouse the interest and emulation of Catholics by telling what the Protestants have done on the West Coast since 1857, while Catholic missions only commenced there in 1885. He concludes his paper thus:

There still remains a broad belt of country along and behind the West Coast, which is heathen, and is therefore ready for Catholic missions. In this belt of country Protestant missions have been at work for years, and each year are increasing and developing their work, occupying the country in all directions. European, and especially British influence, is making itself felt in the Niger-Binué country as far as Sokotoo, Kano, and Lake Chad; and yet, with all this rapid advance of false religion and European power, the Catholic Church has but a few weak and miserably provided missions, scattered along the coast, with four Frenchmen at Lokojah to meet the overwhelming advance of Islam. Happily the French Society of the Holy Ghost has lately established a mission on the left bank of the Lower Niger at a place called Onitsha. I do not know so much about the means and resources of the missions of this Society as I do of those of the Society of African Missions; but of the latter I feel very certain that unless they can be better supported, even in the very necessaries of life, as well as of religion, and also largely increased in number, this great empire of the future must come under the withering influence and subjection either of Mahomet or of Luther.[1]

In 1887 the National African Company received a charter, and changed its name to that of "The Royal Niger Company." The sovereign powers thus conferred, required the Company to organize a judicial system for the territory subject to its

[1] *The Month*, vol. lvii. p. 476.

authority. The long experience of Sir James
Marshall, and his well-known ability in dealing
with the natives, pointed him out as the fittest
person to undertake this work ; and Lord Aberdare, as Governor of the Company, requested him
to accept the position of Chief Justice. He says :

Having retired from that position in the colonial
service on the Gold Coast in 1882, on account of my
health being no longer able to stand the climate, I
declined the honour. I was then asked to go out for a
short time in order to organize a judicial system suitable
to the country. This I did not like to refuse, as the
Council considered me specially fitted by my experience
for a work which I knew was of the greatest importance
for the future of the young empire. I also felt that I
might be of use to the missions, which do so much for
the improvement and conversion of the heathen in
those parts. I therefore accepted, on the understanding
that I should not stay longer than three months, and
should return sooner if I wished.[1]

This short sentence gives no idea of the sacrifice
that it was to him to undertake this expedition.
The method that he adopted to make up his mind
whether or not to run the risk of facing again that
fatal climate is very instructive. He consulted with
his confessor, and it was agreed that he and Lady
Marshall and Father S—— should all make a
novena of special prayer for light, and should each
write down the *pros* and *cons* that occurred to
them through the nine days. Poor Lady Marshall
could see nothing in favour of the expedition, and
everything against it. In fact she is still convinced
that had he not gone out, he would have had
strength to throw off the illness that carried him

---

[1] *Missionary Crusade in Africa*, pp. 6, 7.

off the year after, and his life might have been
considerably prolonged. His own notes, dated
September 4th, 1887, enumerate among the reasons
for going :

Temporal reasons, pecuniary, increase of influence,
benefit to the Company, possible use to the Foreign
Office in settling British rule.

NATIVES.

I may be made the means of establishing better
relations between Europeans and the natives, and may
make the natives go in more heartily for commercial and
other relations with Europeans.

My visit *may* exercise an influence for good by increasing friendly footing and practical justice.

MISSIONS.

I have already been used by God for assisting in
different ways the missions and missionaries, especially at
Lagos, and may be made of further use.

If I go, I accept it as a mission from God, under the
patronage of SS. Ignatius and Francis Xavier, and Blessed
Peter Claver, to serve in any way I can the missions
lately established on the Niger.

If I get a Catholic barrister to go with me for the
purpose of remaining there, as I hope, the effect on
these missions may be great and permanent.

A safe return home will bring many blessings on us all,
temporal and spiritual, if it be God who calls me.

REASONS AGAINST.

The one great reason against it is the break up, even
for a few months, of our happy family ; and the sorrow
and anxiety it will bring upon my dear wife, and also
upon myself.

To escape from this will make it very pleasant not to
go.

It will save us from a bitter trial, which I could not
accept unless I believe this to be a call and an inspiration
from God.

It may all arise from pride and the desire of fame, as well as love of money. Others may do all I have said, as well as I can.

The question is, whether God calls *me* to, at all events, begin the work of promoting His justice out there, and helping the missions.

How am I to know?

CLIMATE AND OTHER DANGERS.

These are apparent to us all. What I feel is, that dangers and death may come at any time, and anywhere. I think a cold wet winter here would be as trying as the dry season out there. And if this is a call from God, I can place myself confidently in His care. Also I have now had experience, which greatly lessens that danger.

There is the risk of failure, and receiving blame instead of praise.

It is evident that the motive of being of use to the missions was uppermost in his mind. Even before he had had the offer made him, the idea had occurred to him. The following note on a loose sheet of paper shows this:

Sunday, Aug. 21st.—This morning at Mass it came surging upon me that I should be asked to go out to the Niger, merely on a visit of inspection; to settle matters, or, it may be, to take out S—— as well and start him. And if so, I should go, if only for the missions' sake.

The following letters, written to his family on the way to the Niger, show clearly the spirit in which he went out; and the contrast between them and the depressed tone of his letters on the last voyage to Africa alone is very striking, and shows how the consciousness that he was making a sacrifice for God's sake lifted him above the natural sorrow of being separated from those he loved so dearly.

To Lady Marshall.

Jan. 20th, 1888.

. . . My aches are not for myself as they were when
I sailed from Plymouth. I am full of high hopes at
what is before me, and were it not for leaving you at
such a time, I should feel more than content. And as it
is, I trust to your keeping a good heart, and sharing my
confidence that I am called to a high and also a pleasant
duty. So be brave, my own dear wife, and let us each
throw ourselves cheerfully into our work. .. . .. I have
placed myself as well as you and the dear chicks in the
keeping of the Sacred Heart of Jesus. You will, I
know, do the same, and all will be well. Before this
reaches you, a telegram will, I hope, have told you that
we are off, and God will bless you.

[From his Journal.]

S.S. Roquelle, Jan. 21*st,* 1888.

The first day at sea is always a misery, but the *Roquelle*
was as steady as a house on shore, and at luncheon I
found we had a decidedly nice set of passengers. I was
on the captain's left, and next me came two majors of
the 1st West, both of whom claimed former acquaintance
with me. Opposite was Dr. Crutch and his step-daughter.
He seems to have been a traveller from his youth all over
the world, but especially in Iceland and Norway, where
his daughter comes from. Next them sat Lieutenant
Gordon, lately of the navy, who is going to the Niger
as an officer of the constabulary. Next him is a man
who has seen a deal of civil service in British Honduras,
and was once private secretary to Sir Robert Harley,
and is now going to Lagos to join the constabulary.
Kane and the purser complete our table. At the other
the "palm oil" element prevails, but of a good class,
and also a young man named Storcy, going to Madeira,
whose father, as M.P. for Sunderland, has done good
work for Home Rule, and therefore he and I have
become fast friends. There is also one of the Niger
Company's agents named Lister.

After lunch I wrote a farewell letter to Alice and the

chicks and a post-card to Libby, which the pilot took off.
The weather cleared up a bit and I quite enjoyed the
sea-breezes, after being cooped up in London, though
my heart ached at being torn away from there. At
dinner I was very pleased to find the saloon quite bright
and pretty, and so well lighted that it looked quite
cheerful; and I saw that I should be able to read in it
easily of an evening, which has not often been the case.
The company also was evidently much above the average.
Dr. Crutch talks incessantly about any part of the world,
and any subject. Lieutenant Gordon does the same,
and when there is a struggle as to which voice is to
prevail, the lieutenant generally wins. He has his
sailor's yarns and the doctor his traveller's stories, and
they vie as to capping each other with the best story.
After dinner the smoking-room was well filled, and I
certainly never had such an amusing, pleasant first
evening at sea. Generally the purser and doctor of the
ship enliven the wretched victims with their jokes and
witticisms ; but they were but listeners, whilst Lieutenant
Gordon kept us immensely amused with stories and
tricks at cards, at which he is quite the conjurer.
Altogether, I was thankful at the contrast this start was
with what I had from Plymouth in January, 1881. I
then went out on deck and found a splendid moon
shining, with the stars most brilliant, and though it was
cold, with a strong breeze from the west, the ship kept
quite steady, and we were past Holyhead. Kane has
to share my cabin at present, but he is a pleasant
companion for it.

Sunday, 22nd.—After a sound sleep I woke, feeling
quite rested, and the ship had gone on quite steady. It
was not so cold, but after passing Jusca about 6 a.m.,
and getting exposed to the Atlantic, there was a considerable swell, which I rather enjoyed, though some
others did not. It was fine, but some nasty fogs came on
occasionally. The wind went round to the N.W., so we
had the try-sails up and afterwards the square sails. In
the afternoon the sea became shorter, which made me a
wee bit uncomfortable, but for a very short time. Kane
and others succumbed for a time. The ship is a parti-

cularly steady one, and the cabins being amidships the
motion is but little felt, even when the bows of the ship
are up and down in style.

Dr. Crutch and the lieutenant keep up to the mark,
and at dinner the subject was "food." They kept pace
with each other up to frogs, snails, and other things;
but the doctor finished with saying he had eaten *human*
flesh and liked it, and had no scruple about it. This was
a floorer for the lieutenant, and the subject was changed.
In the smoking-room afterwards the stories went on, but
the lieutenant had the most talk, including a history of
his grandfather, who had been the last Governor of
Greenwich Hospital. He lost a leg in action and had
a good pension for it. Afterwards his wooden leg was
shot in another action in America and he put in a claim
for the loss of another leg, and (so said the lieutenant)
got it.

I got through the day very well, reading, and exami-
ning one of my trunks, to get out things that I required.
The deck was pleasant, except when the fogs came on,
and the sea air is most refreshing and invigorating.
Personally, I think I shall in many ways enjoy the voyage,
and certainly my lungs enjoy the air. I did not turn in
till 10.30.

22nd, Monday.—Another good night, and ship steady.
Bright sun, slight breeze, and so mild I was glad to dress
with the port open, and found my great coat too warm
on deck. I am busy in one of my books of African
travel. The captain (Hely) told me, that he had heard
that Dr. Crutch's experience in eating human flesh
consisted in his cutting off his thumb, after a gun accident, and then having it cooked and eating it himself.
Is it cannibalism to eat one's own self? After dinner
Lieutenant Gordon gave us some capital conjuring tricks
in the smoking-room, after which the Norwegian girl
played the piano in the saloon, accompanying songs.
Kane sang well. The saloon was quite a pretty sight,
and I certainly never had so pleasant a voyage so far,
especially as we are making such good way, and if we
continue as at present we should reach Madeira on
Friday afternoon.

Wednesday, 25th.—We certainly are having a most lovely voyage. Yesterday was cloudy with a stiff breeze from the east, which filled the sails and kept us going right merrily. There was a bit of a sea running, but not more than I like, and the ship is so heavily laden that she did not roll much, and I did three long walks on the small poop deck at the stern, which I can generally get to myself. In the evening the sky cleared and the wind fell, and the bright moon and stars were lovely. I could see the horizon all round, and altogether it was so beautiful that I did not turn in till eleven o'clock, which was midnight at home. No one is sea-sick now, and the flow of talk and stories greater than ever. The Lagos officer has had a cold and been sick, but now adds much to the yarns, and Dr. Crutch is comparatively subdued, especially when the lieutenant is on the talk with a voice that drowns all others. But many of his stories now come out for the second time. The talk in the smoking-room was very interesting, being about all parts of the world, as well as the African Coast, about which Major Ellis, who is on board, gave information, especially as to its ancient history, which was very interesting. He writes books about the Coast, which are a sort of parody on things as they are ; and I wish he would write more in the way he talked last night. It was so mild that I wore no great coat on the deck. This morning we are in a blaze of warm sunshine, and every one sitting about on deck, as though it were summer. I wonder if you are all shivering with east wind and choked with fogs. Two ships have been in sight, making three since we left the Channel. We are going very fast for this line, and seem sure to reach Madeira on Friday.

Thursday, 26th.—Yesterday kept lovely to the last, and so warm that I have left off warm underclothing to-day and feel more comfortable. In the evening we had singing, in which Kane again excelled. I quite wished I had some of my songs with me. The rage for the Canary Islands certainly has improved the class of passengers very much ; and, putting aside my home anxieties, I have really enjoyed the voyage so far. I feel immensely the better for it, and am hungry for every meal.

We are due at Madeira to-morrow forenoon, so I will
close this account for the present, and am glad to assure
you all that so far everything has gone right merrily, and
that I am in excellent health and spirits.

To his Son.

S.S. Roquelle, Off Lisbon, Jan. 25*th*, 1888.

MY VERY DEAR BOY,—I wish I could have written to
you each day since I sailed, but there was no use in
doing so on the wide ocean where I could not see even
a bird to ask it to carry one to you. But we are now
getting on so fast that we expect to reach Madeira on
Friday instead of the usual day, Saturday, so I am
beginning to write my letters. It is quite warm to-day,
like summer, with bright sun and a calm sea, and so
far God has indeed heard the prayers of my dear three
at home, and given me a beautiful voyage. I am writing
an account of the voyage which mammy will tell you
about. I have seen no land since we left the Mersey,
sea all round each day, and scarcely a ship. We have
seen two to-day and one before, and that is all I have
seen. A lot of gulls followed close for a time, picking
up what they could from the ship, but they do not like
to go far from land, so we have the sea all to ourselves
as far as the horizon in a great circle around us. To-day
I watched a ship coming up gradually above the horizon,
like in your geography book. I often think of you, my
own dear Bernard, and it helps me much to think of
what a comfort you will be when I am away both to
mammy and Mary. You are very young; but, for all
that, I know you will be a great help to mammy, and
will keep her from getting sad and too anxious about me.
Many boys would only add to her troubles; but I do
thank God, because I can feel sure you will do all you
can to help her, and to keep her cheerful and happy.
I hope you are at Eastbourne to-day, or going there, and
I only wish I could give you the weather we have got
here. I shall be glad when you can settle down again
to lessons and regular habits, which have been so broken
up by poor little Mary's illness. I am sure you believe

that I only left you all because I felt it was my duty to go, both for the work given me to do, and for the good of my family.   In the end, I feel sure it will add to the happiness of us all.   I say my Rosary, and the prayers you say for me, each night on deck; and the nights have been so lovely, with the moon and stars shining bright, that I have felt in a grand open-air church, especially when I get a part of the deck all to myself.   I like, too, to sing the "Hail, thou Star of ocean" quietly when on the ocean, and of course I always unite myself with my precious three in the Sacred Heart of Jesus.   Each day, at twelve o'clock, the captain and two officers of the ship look at the sun through an instrument called a quadrant, by which they are able to tell exactly where we are, and so to calculate how many miles the ship has gone since twelve o'clock in the previous day.   Yesterday they found we had sailed 247 miles, to-day it was 252, which is at the rate of 10½ miles each hour.   I shall post this at Madeira, which I dare say you have found on the map.   I do not like to think that each day is taking me further from you all, but I must get to the end before I can begin to come back again.   God ever bless you, my bonnie boy!   I hope you will give me a long account of all you do each week; and you must keep merry, and make mother be merry too, and then your old dad will be merry also, especially as he cannot have the immense pleasure of coming back home without first going away from it.   I keep your loving face in my mind as I parted from it at Euston, and I pray God to keep you happy and well when I am away.

Ever, my dear Bernard,
Your loving father,
JAMES MARSHALL.

To Lady Marshall.

S.S. Roquelle, Wed., Feb. 8th, 1888.
After a very pleasant day at Sierra Leone, we are again at sea, and very refreshing it is as the cool breeze still keeps on, and clouds as well.   These parts have had rain lately, which is very unusual.   I left a very

hurried letter for you at Sierra Leone, to follow the
budget I sent by the Hamburg boat; but now, in the
retirement of the ship, I can write you a fuller account of
all I did at Freetown. On Monday morning I was
visited by Mr. Stuart, the collector of customs, and
Mr. Alldridge, who is now agent for Swanzy's, and who
put his house at my disposal. I went off for the shore
in the customs' boat, carrying a letter for me from Sir
S. Rowe, offering me all the hospitality he could give.
However, I went straight to Daniel's quarters, where I
knew I could be quite at my ease. I found him at his
toilet, which is evidently as important a ceremony as
ever, but he was very pleased to see me. . . . Every
corner, chair, and article in his house is as neat and
precise as ever. I clamoured for breakfast, and was glad
to find he had to breakfast as early as half-past nine, in
order to be ready for court. We had some fowl nicely
cooked, and some chops or cutlets of the West African
diminutive style, and I ate all I could get; but, being
still hungry, was dismayed at the boy next giving me a
finger-glass. All I could do was to take a big coarse
banana, and attack a bottle of biscuits. Kane joined
us here, and I sent off a polite note to the Governor,
telling him I was breakfasting with Daniel, and engaged
to dine with Mr. Alldridge, but would call on him later.
Back came a kind reply asking me to go out with him at
five, or he feared he might miss me. . . . Daniel then
went to court, leaving Kane and me in his room.

Happily a strong Harmattan breeze struck up, which we
enjoyed, and I opened the window as much as possible,
and wrote to you and had a smoke. Between me and
the wind, Daniel's papers and other things got somewhat
upset; and I had a capital laugh at the dear fellow on
his return, as I watched him putting things straight, and
consigning bits of paper to the waste-basket. It was
now near two, and I had to tell him we must have some
lunch. He at once ordered some, and said he did not
often take any, but would do so too, as he felt hungry.
So we three sat down, and presently the boy brought in
two poached eggs on very small pieces of toast. He
said some fowl was coming, so Kane said he would wait

for it. I therefore swallowed one egg in about two mouthfuls, whilst poor Daniel fiddled away at the other. Presently, in came a leg and wing of a fowl, the size of which you know. I could have eaten the whole of it, and still wanted more. I asked for some bread, declining the fowl for Kane's sake. Daniel took the tiny loaf or rather roll, and cut off two or three thin delicate slices. Kane's face of amusement made me know he twigged my position, and he quietly cut off a big lump which I devoured. Daniel gave us some mineral water in bottle, which he said is much used there. I resolved to take a case with us; but, after I had consumed a considerable quantity, he informed me that one great advantage was its purgative powers. I remonstrated with him for not having told me this before, and my nocturnal experience made me resolve *not* to take a case with me. The dear fellow has a very small appetite, and though I impressed upon him he must excuse my very different state, and Kane also, he did not seem a bit to realize the real truth of the case.

At five, a wheel-chair arrived from Government House, and I proceeded there, where I was received by Rowe in the most pleasant and charming way. He was at his very best, genuinely glad to see me, asked very nicely after you, and saying in the neatest way how glad he would have been to see you gracing Government House again, though at the same time how glad he was you were not with me. He introduced the Queen's Advocate to me, and after some champagne we sallied forth. He politely saw me into the wheel-chair, which I preferred to a hammock. In fact, if it had been *you* he could not have been more courteous and polite, and at the same time so friendly that I was quite at my ease with him. He and the Q. A. then got into their hammocks, and off we went. He made the man drawing my chair to hold the hand of one of the front bearers of his hammock, so that we might keep close together; and then we made the most amusing progress through the native town and market that you can imagine, as you know the man and his queer body-guard. I had never seen this part of the town, and it was most

interesting and amusing. The streets were crowded
with the natives, chattering and chaffering at their stores,
and numberless baskets, tables, and stalls covered with
peppers, eggs, fruits, and all sorts of eatables. A crowd
of urchins ran after and about us, and though the
reception of the Governor was not what one would call
respectful, it was amusing and in some places hearty
and certainly noisy. The women started something like
"Ebba" as the salutation, and off went the Governor's
hat; and if the salutings were strong, he placed his hat
on his knees and smiled, which caused shouts of laughing. Every now and then, a sturdy woman would utter
a loud comment in an unknown tongue, which raised
peals of laughing. We passed, through the town, to a
part round the bay, where there are splendid mango-
trees, palms, silk-cottons, and wrecks of gardens and
houses, showing it used formerly to be a fashionable
resort. We came to a broken-down property belonging
to the Government, which he wished to visit, and there
we alighted, and I wished I could have sketched His
Excellency in his baggy breeches and queer get up.

The view from the place we got to was most lovely,
and we said, What a glorious place it would be but for
the climate. It was dark when we returned; and,
instead of saying good-bye at the avenue to Government
House, he insisted on going with me to Mr. Alldridge's
door, and there left me. He was most amusing all the
way, just as he used to be when he paid us those evening
visits at Accra. I enjoyed the dinner at Mr. Alldridge's.
His house is furnished in a way not often seen in these
parts, and the table with its bright flowers, frangipani,
lilies, &c., glass, and spotless cleanliness, was very refreshing after s.s. meals, and the dinner was excellent as
well as plentiful, so that I had a good square meal.
Gore of the Commissariat was there. Alldridge's house
is charming, and when he offered me a large bed-room
furnished most tastefully and appropriately, with bath-
room and every luxury, I wished I had brought a change
on shore; but as I had not, after a pleasant evening I
went back to the *Roquelle* with Kane. The night was
horribly close and hot, and it was difficult to sleep.

I took occasional wanders to get cool, but then got frightened of *chills*, so bore it as well as I could in my bunk.

I was glad to get up and go on shore. We then visited the missions, where the Fathers received me *very* warmly. They then showed us the new church, which is large, and, for Africa, handsome, with stained-glass windows. We then went to the convent, where the Superior is French and all the Sisters Irish, but not one of them had ever seen me before. The change in the mission since I was last there is as marked as it is delightfuL I thought they would never make head against the degraded numberless sects which have debased the natives for so long. But I hope I am quite wrong. Even here it is becoming to be, as on the Gold Coast and Lagos, that the Catholic missionaries are *respected*, and numbers of converts made ; and it was a treat to go through the school-rooms and see the classes of clean modest girls, with the Sisters, at their work of love. The new church is none too big ; and, a few days ago, at some large Protestant missionary gathering, a young man rose up before the Bishop and minister and said that the only missionaries worthy of respect and who worked truly were the Catholics. He is a rising man of influence among the natives, and the effect was great, but his speech was *not* reported in the local papers. The Fathers said that there was a very great change altogether, and that now they were making real progress ; and that, instead of abuse and insult, they were now treated with general courtesy, and that numbers now asked for information about the Faith, instead of being content with the lies told them.

Kane breakfasted with Daniel, but I thought it safer to go to Mr. Alldridge, where I had plenty even for my appetite. He supplied me with a nice pipe in a case to take the place of the one stolen at Teneriffe. He also had some spectacles in his store, gold ones ; so, curious to say, for the first time I have got *gold* specs., and got them in West Africa. I went at twelve to call on the Governor, and fortunately found him going to breakfast ; so I sat down beside him, and he chatted away as pleasantly and amusingly as before, and had out the champagne again. His table was bright with flowers, and everything as nice as could be—so different from Accra. He was most hearty to the last, came to the stairs with me, and it was all I could do to get away on my legs instead of in a chair with a body-guard. . . . After warm good-byes and many good wishes for success and safe return, from natives as well as whites, I went on board, feeling very happy because your good news kept everything bright, and about three o'clock we were again underweigh in a good breeze. I was charmed to be afloat again, and felt as hearty and strong as ever.

Thursday, Feb. 9th.—We arrived at Monrovia yesterday at half-past six. The voyage there was very pleasant, good breeze and deep blue sea. We have lost the two majors, so the company is not as pleasant as it was. . . . After anchoring here the breeze died away, and it became very still and hot. The Lagos man, Millson, has been ill with a diphtheria style of attack, but is about again, and after dinner he again played the piano, and accompanied Kane and others with their songs. Kane sings capitally, and it was very pleasant for us on deck to have this concert. It was so hot I stayed on deck till past eleven, and then went to bed. I had a restless, broken night with the close heat, and pernicious insects biting my ankles, and was much tempted to take a Madeira sofa on deck, but resisted. The thermometer did not go below 81°, but I got some sleep and feel all right, though the heat is oppressive. It has clouded over, which is a comfort, and I hear thunder. It is now raining hard, and everything seems cooler and fresher.

Friday, 10th.—It is not much like the dry season hereabouts. At six yesterday, after an intensely hot afternoon, a thunder-storm set in with a deluge of rain and high wind. It was intensely dark; but there were such constant flashes of bright lightning, that one could scarcely say whether light or darkness prevailed. It lasted for a long time, and I thought how horribly frightened you would have been. Happily the breeze from the sea kept on during the night, and came into my cabin, and I slept well and am much refreshed. It rained a good deal during the night, and about four another tornado set in, and I was roused by the rain coming in upon my bunk. Once also I was woke up by the ship stopping; and, on looking out, I was rather scared by seeing a bright light which seemed just ahead. But I soon made out that it was a big solitary star, and the captain told me it was Venus, which has been so specially bright this year. This morning we called off Grand Cess for Kroo-boy passengers, but there were none for any of the ports we call at, so they had to go off again, taking to the water in their clever way. One old fellow had got a pipe of baccy, and in he went and swam to his canoe, without stopping his smoke all the way.

Grand Bassa, Sunday, Quinquagesima, Feb. 11th. — We keep crawling along in true coast style, and I am now very weary of the voyage. The captain gives me free use of his cabin, which is a comfort at times. Last night I sat a long time with him on deck, each occupying a very nice kind of Madeira sofa, which I got there, of a more comfortable shape than the old style. At last he said : "This is Saturday night." "Wives and Sweethearts," say I, the old ship-toast on that night. "Come along and drink it," says he. "Certainly," I reply, and we go to his cabin. But I made the toast, "Wives and Children, God bless them," to which he heartily responded, as he is evidently devoted to both. We anchored for the night at Grand Bassa, a French place, but with a large Swanzy factory, for which we are now slowly discharging cargo. To-morrow, I suppose, we must get as far as Elmina; and, as we have cargo for there, I intend to land, which will be a nice break, and give me more to write about. I fear there is not much chance of my landing at Lagos, unless I stayed there for the next steamer, which I cannot do on the outward voyage.

I will close this letter, in case I post it at Elmina, and will get letters ready for the dear pets.

Ever your loving,

J. M.

We have had several rattling tornadoes. I have written a paper on Sierra Leone to the *Catholic Press*, so look out for it.

I

S.S. Roquelle, Feb. 14th, 1888.

I have been to Elmina and Cape Coast, and have
much reason to be gratified with the warm reception I
met with. . . . We arrived at Elmina early yesterday,
and I landed in the Government boat, with Kane,
Gordon, and Dr. Bate, the naval man, who is a great
favourite with us all. The boatmen paddled and sang as
of old, and Kane was charmed. The sea was as quiet as
it ever is, and we were skilfully landed. We made for
the Castle, and there were lots of the Houssas sitting in
groups about the parade-ground. Some of them evidently recognized me, and soon all were on their legs to
salute me. We passed in by the drawbridge and port-
cullis, and the guard turned out and stood to arms—so
like old times. Cecil Dudley has left, and gone to
Cyprus; but I found Firminger in command, and
another officer, Newnham, whom I also knew, and they
received me very cheerily, and asked us all to breakfast
at eleven.

I then made my way to the missions with Kane,
and on our way passed the house of Chief Andoh,
the principal, and my favourite, chief. He was holding
his court, surrounded by his officials and others, and
hearing a case. I told Kane to look, but the chief looked
up and saw me. He gave an exclamation, jumped up
from his seat, lowered his cloth from his shoulder—the
native salutation—and rushed to me without any cere-
monial, and shook me warmly by the hand, with words
of hearty welcome. He then said something to his court, I
suppose to explain so unusual a proceeding, but many of
them knew me, and I had to do a deal of hand-shaking.
We then went on to the mission-house, which stands well
on the top of a hill, and is a house exposed to every
breeze, and in which they have some chance of living.
Father Pellatt and three others received me as an old
and welcome friend, though I had never met any of
them. It is marvellous the progress they have made,
and are making. The people are very well disposed
towards them, and the Wesleyans are nowhere against
them. On Sundays the three school-rooms are opened
up for Mass, the altar being shut off on school-days, like

it used to be at Lagos ; and they told me that numbers cannot get in. They have over one hundred and fifty boys at school, whilst the Wesleyans have only about fifty, and one of the native Wesleyan ministers has been converted. If they had but money to build a proper church, and found missions in places where they are asked to do so, a great work would be done. . . .

Father Pellatt then took us to the Sisters, who have the house nearest to the Castle, just on the other side of the bridge and river. The Superior is Sister Claire, one of our old Lagos friends, who, poor thing, looks a bit of shrivelled parchment, but says she has good health. Another Sister had seen me at Lagos, when I was last there. There are four of them, but my chief interest was in the Irish girl who went out with Father Moreau, four or five years ago. Father Keily visited the party on board at Plymouth, and spoke to her in French, but observing a very Irish accent in her reply, tried English, and found great amusement in the result. She is *so* pretty, I may say beautiful, a fine refined face, with charming eyes and manner, a delightful example of a good Irish girl. Those who were then with her are all dead, but she keeps bright and happy, though she has evidently given her *life* for the negroes. Kane tried his French with Sister Claire, but the Irish girl told me she didn't think he talked French well, and that she could talk it much better herself. They have a good many girls, but there is a great prejudice in Elmina against girls being educated. We then went to the Castle, and had an excellent breakfast in the round-room, adjoining the Governor's quarters. These are quite dismantled, and the furniture carried off to Accra. The head-quarters of the constabulary are going to be removed to Christiansborg Castle. There has been no rain in these parts, but the day was cloudy, with a good Harmattan breeze. . . .

When we were at the Fathers, I received a messenger from Chief Andoh with followers, one of whom carried his cane, which beats mine, as it has a handsome *gold* top. He informed me that the chief wished to pay me a visit, to bid me welcome. I replied that I should be very pleased to see him at the Castle. About twelve he arrived, and I received him in the court-house, taking my seat on the bench as of old. He brought one of the other chiefs, and though they did not come in *full* state, with sword-bearers, drummers, &c., still it was quite enough to let Kane see with how much dignity a real chief could conduct himself. They wore handsome silk cloths of native work, with gold ornaments and aggry beads, and Chief Andoh rose and made a speech to me himself, and not through the linguist, as in *full* cere-monial. I was really happy at seeing it all again, and at Kane having so good an opportunity of seeing for himself what I have told him about the chiefs. Our inter-preter was a good one, as he gave the poetical parable turns which they, like the Eastern nations, use so much. I wish . . . you could have heard it all, without my having to tell it, for I know you would have been as gratified as I was, and it seems rather egotistical to try and repeat it. He welcomed me back to Elmina, where they had never expected to see me again, but where they would always remember me with affection. The prettiest part I remember was, that my memory remained like a sweet song in the mouths of the people. In reply, I told him how glad I was to see him and his people again, that I always looked back with pleasure on the days when I sat there in court with the chiefs; that I never expected to have been there again, but that I had been asked to go to the Niger, to establish courts of the same sort, where I could sit in friendship with the chiefs, but that I was too old to stay there, and had therefore brought a friend who would remain as Judge. I then introduced Kane, who spoke some friendly words to them, which they much liked, and so did I. Chief Andoh then gave him a speech of welcome, and told him that, if he wished to succeed, he should follow in my footsteps, and act with the people as I had done. He then made me a farewell speech, which so went to my heart, that I felt tears gathering in my eyes. He asked that the Great God might watch over me, and take care of me, and give me success in my journey, and that God would take me safe back to my country and family. I was a little choking in my reply, and told him I thanked him, and that when I got home, I would tell my wife and children of all he had said. I never was more impressed with the simple dignity and eloquence of this fine heathen chief, and only wish there were more like him. Kane was much impressed, and I was very glad he was present.

After this, I found the *Roquelle* had gone off, and was at Cape Coast, so, as it was cloudy and breezy, we all agreed to walk, and at 3.30 we started. As we went through the town, I received many a salutation, and was not a little pleased at this visit to Elmina. We did the march in two hours and a quarter, and I kept up the pace the whole way, and though precious glad to get to Cape Coast, I was not a bit done up. Lieutenant Gordon was the most distressed, and said my pace nearly did for him. About two miles from Cape Coast, we were met by the D. C., Mr. Rayner, a barrister, whom I coached up in the place before he came out, about four months ago. Cape Coast looked much the same. We passed the cemetery, and along the road which you will remember. Every now and then a native looked with surprise, made an exclamation, and then laughed, and made me welcome in some way or another. I saw my house on the hill, looking much as it always did. Presently we passed the Wesleyan mission, where some of the ministers were in the garden. I saw them talk together as we passed, and there my welcome was doubtless of a different character. I dare say I shall be served up again in the next number of their local paper. Rayner's quarters are new, and close to Gothic House. He is a total abstainer, and we soon emptied all his lime-drink jugs and filter. It was getting late, and I knew boatmen do not like going off after dark, so we went on to the Castle, where we called on Major Wilton, now in command there. He was my D. C. in Woodcock's days, and I sat upon him occasionally. He stood us whiskies and sodas, which were refreshing. We then went to the beach, where I found one of my old Cape Coast chiefs waiting to see me. He told me he was the only one left whom I knew. Attah, whose elephant's tail you have, Armoah, who, I think, made your gold chain, Thompson and

Robertson, who wore European clothes and tall hats,
and looked very common, all dead and gone. He hoped
I would land on my way back, so that the present chiefs
might give me a reception. But, as you know, the
chiefs who have for long been under English rule are a
very inferior class to the Elminas, who have only had
that doubtful blessing since 1873. We were carried into
the surf-boat as of old, and paddled out by a very fine
set of men, who sang lustily all the way, and paddled
hard. We all got safely on board, full of spirits (I mean
animal spirits), and I felt as well as I ever did since we
left.

On the previous day I was much depressed with a
sick headache, not severe, but depressing. I went to bed
at eight, and woke up all right, and the day on shore
and the walk have made me quite spry. The rains have
not been here at all, and to-day is bright and hot, but
with the sea-breeze, so I do not suppose we shall have any
more. We are now at Appam, and have to do Winnebah before Accra, so we shall not get there till some time
to-morrow. I will have this ready to post there, but
cannot write any other letters, not even to the chicks, but
tell them I send them lots of love and kisses. . . . So
far everybody and everything seem to tell me I am right
in coming, so keep cheery, . . . and soon we shall all be
happy together again. . . .

Feb. 15*th.*—We were so long at Appam yesterday, that
we are this morning only at Winnebah, but expect to get
to Accra in good time. It is Ash Wednesday, and I
sincerely wish I could dine off lentil soup and fish. . . .
I am so thankful the voyage is coming to an end. Kane
agrees with me that our Lent is quite cut out for us.

Evening.—I have been ashore at Accra, but the
Governor, Dr. M'Carthy, and Mr. Pagau are all away, so
I found no one I care for, or who care for me. But I
went to New Site, now called Victoriaburg, and was
much interested in seeing the old place, and the house
where I was so happy with you. I found young Griffith
at the Q. A. house, and he was very nice and cordial.
He is going to Jamaica, and promised to call on you
when he gets home. Our house looks very dingy and

dreary, cut up into three rooms, and a square room
built out on the sea-side, which is nice in itself, but
makes the sitting-room dark and close. I looked up
Mrs. Andoh, who was very pleased to see me. Chiefs
Adjabin Ankrah and Cleland are both dead. Your telegram was sent off to me, and was deeply interesting. . . .

S.S. Roquelle, Forcados River, Feb. 20th, 1888.
My cablegram would let you know that we not only
landed at Lagos, but remained a night there. I was
very pleased to see the place again, and Moloney received
me not only cordially, but I may say affectionately. He
sent out a kind note of invitation by the branch steamer,
including Kane, and when we arrived off Gaiser's wharf,
the Governor's boat came off for us. Moloney was
very pleased to hear of his wife and child, and was very
cordial with Kane also. . . . Presently we had the
luxury of a capital breakfast, which I did great justice to,
as I had no difficulty in restraining my appetite at the
ship breakfast before we left. Our captain and all the
passengers left came on shore, as we were to go out
again at four. But after breakfast the agent sent to say
we were to stay till the next day. A second collar was
all I brought on shore, but Moloney took care of us,
and I occupied our old room. After breakfast, I went
with Kane to the mission, and to my deep disappointment found that Father Chausse was away at Topo, the
farm, in attendance on a dying Sister. They buried an
Irish Sister a few days ago. This quite spoiled my visit,
for though the four we saw were very pleased to see me,
they were all strangers. We also visited the church,
which I was glad to see. Afterwards Moloney took us
in his steam-launch to Ebute Metta, where he has
commenced a garden for experimenting on trees, &c.
I liked to be on the lagoon again, and could study the
Marina well. Young Jarbet is unfortunately at Badagry,
but Millson will relieve him, and he will go home, as
he is far from well.

I then went with Moloney to Mass at nine, which
was a great pleasure, such a contrast in every way to our
former experiences. The church is large and airy, the

singing simple and really good, and the congregation large and really picturesque. The poor Sisters still struggle on in their old house, so it is no wonder they die off. After Mass, I called on E. Richards, as he is laid up with liver without fever. He has a nice house, and is going to act as Judge during Smalman Smith's absence. Moloney spoke highly of him in *every* way. . . . Moloney volunteered to write to you. . . . I was quite touched with his anxiety about me, and the way he urged me not to stay long. I saw J. P. L. Davis and his young daughter, Stella. Our old house remains in ruins, having been in constant litigation between J. P. L. and Sykes, but the Government has now taken it, and lodged the purchase-money in court for whomsoever can prove his title to it.

At two o'clock we went on board the branch steamer. Two of the Fathers came out with us, a French and an Irishman, and I got to know them better in consequence. The bar was quite quiet each day. I saw the remains of the *Nellie* in Lagos, in which we were nearly lost. How I thought of that day as we went in![1] The transfer from one steamer to another was as disagreeable as ever, and there was a deal of drinking on the branch steamer as we came out, so I was glad to get on board the *Roquelle*, and get under weigh. We had a fine breeze, which kept up at night, and I slept well. This morning we anchored in the Forcados River, a very fine estuary in connection with the Niger, which, curious to say, has never been occupied, but will soon, I expect, be scrambled for. The bar is better than at any other months, and is much more direct to the Niger than Akassa. It is now used as the place for loading and unloading Lagos and Benin cargoes, as the branch steamer can come alongside, and so take in the cargo much more quickly. This is what we are now doing, and dreary work it is. I hope we shall finish to-morrow, but it seems probable if the *Bonny* comes to-morrow that we may be kept another day transhipping *gin* from her. But, as you know, there is no use fuming or fretting, and thank God I am quite

[1] See p. 76.

well, and so is Kane. My delight at receiving your
Lagos telegram was immense in relieving my anxiety
about Mary's eye.   I was tortured with fears lest there
might be some serious injury to the poor child's eye;
but now I hope she will soon be all right again, and that
you will all keep merry and well.

I shall soon be at work now, and shall know better
what can be done, but I am sure that whatever can be
done or has to be done, will be carried out by Kane as
well as (and probably better) than by me.

21st, *Tuesday.*—The steamer which is taking in the
Lagos cargo from us is going off. there to-day, so I will
send this by her to be posted for the next homeward
ship. We are all in hopes that the *Bonny* will not
arrive, in which case we will sail to-day, and get to
Akassa in the morning. It was very hot last night,
thermometer at 85°, enough even for you! I wandered
on deck to get cool, and found a delightful sea-breeze
blowing, but I feared a chill, and went in the smoking-
room, and slept there for a bit, and then finished in my
cabin. Give my love to dear Bernard and Mary, and
tell them there is a great trade doing here in parrots,
but I want to get mine nearer my Niger home.   These
weary cargo days make me very home-sick, but to-morrow
I hope we shall be in our own territory. . . .

I like Kane more and more, and feel most thankful
at having him as my companion. His watchfulness to
do anything he can for me would win your heart, and
I can talk to him quite freely and unreservedly. I feel
as anxious over his health as about my own. I suppose
communication with you will now become more uncertain,
but occasional cablegrams will let each of us know how
things are going on. God bless you all! If I feel
getting at all shaky, I will be off home; but, so far,
I am perfectly well, and am well spotted with prickly
heat, which is a good though trying sign. . . . I am
sending an article on the Elmina Mission to the *Catholic
Press* with this.

Asaba, River Niger, March 10th, 1888.
MY OWN DEAR BERNARD,—Here is Saturday, March
10th, and I have not yet received a single home letter

since we left Liverpool. Last night a river steamer
came up from Akassa, and Mr. Kane and I were both
all agog for letters, but no, when she left Akassa, the
steamer which sailed from Liverpool the Saturday after
ours, had not arrived. She went ashore at Sierra Leone,
which caused great delay. It will, I fear, be quite
another week before another Niger steamer comes up,
but I should think she would bring two sets of letters.
There is no steamer for England due at Akassa for
another fortnight, but we are advised to send down
letters by every steamer that leaves here, as there is no
depending on when they come or go or reach Akassa.
So, as the steamer is going back on Monday morning,
I will get a letter ready for you, my bonnie boy. Happily,
she brought me a telegram which ought to have reached
me at Akassa on the day she left, but I suppose it was
sent over from Brass too late to catch us. The message
comforted me greatly. . . . I shall have to tell you
most about my Niger life when I get home, but I will
tell you something about it now. I did not like Akassa
at all. The house and buildings are on a very flat piece
of ground very little above the river on one side, and
swamps on the other, and, oh my! it *did* rain, and one
night there was a furious tornado, but I think I have
told you this before. The mouth of the Niger there,
which is called the "Nun," is like an enormous lake
full of large islands, and when we sailed off, I found
these were not real islands with forests growing on them,
but only immense masses of mangroves which grow right
out of the water to the height of big trees. They have
not one big trunk, but lots of slender ones, and if a
branch grows out far it drops down more roots. There
is a clumsy drawing of them, but of course they are
covered with foliage, and it looks rather pretty. We
dodged in and out of these islands for some time before
we got into the actual channel of the Niger itself, and
after a bit there were signs of large bushes of palm
leaves mixed among the mangroves, showing there was
some soil beginning. Gradually we came to trees, and
the mangroves got fewer, and before we anchored for the
night, we were beyond these, and saw forests on each

side. The river there was not as wide as the Thames at Putney, but it is very low just now. Next morning, March 2nd, I was up at five, and it was quite a cool morning, and I had a rug over me when we sailed. The country was flat, and the banks beautiful with grand trees and forest, and we also began to pass small villages, where the people farm. On the 3rd we got to where the river was much wider, but also shallower, and that night we anchored close to the bank, and though I slept under mosquito curtains, I was miserable from being bitten by sand-flies, especially on my feet.

Next day we stuck fast at twelve o'clock, and did not get off until eight next morning (Sunday), and I had another bad night. We now had begun to see *alligators* lying on the banks, and some of those on board took shots at them, but without effect, until we passed a young one on a bank near us, and he was killed dead on the spot. The river now was more like a lot of lakes, and I was much interested on seeing *hippopotami*. One cannot see much of them, only their noses and parts of their great heads. Nobody hit any of them, and they sink very quickly when alarmed; but, as they cannot stay long under water, they have to come up again, though generally some way off. It is very awkward for a native in a canoe if a hippopotamus rises under his boat. I wondered if any of them belonged to the family of that celebrated one, of which Mary Ann used to teach you about at St. Marychurch as having difficulty in getting in at the door of the ark. On Sunday night, when at anchor, it was so hot I could not sleep in my cabin, and sat on deck. It was very dark, and I saw vivid lightning, and presently I heard a roaring noise coming nearer and nearer, and soon a violent tornado broke upon us. I then quickly retired, and out jumped the captain with a tornado of his own, in the shape of scolding the watchmen for not having put up the canvas curtains round our raised deck. It got cool at once, and in a few minutes I was fast asleep through all the noise. We arrived at Onitsha on the morning of the 5th, and went on shore to look at a house, as we found *our* one at Asaba was not *nearly* finished; but, much as we should have liked to live near the mission, we knew all our work, stores, and furniture, and everything were at Asaba. So we went on there, about twenty minutes' sail, and found this house, and took possession of it.

Mid-Lent Sunday, March 11th.—And now, my dear boy, we have been to our first Mass, and I thank God for having been allowed to visit this new missionary work on the Niger. Having had our early breakfast of tea, toast, thin captains, and potted meat about seven, we went down to the river, and got into a canoe. In the centre, where it is broadest, there were two chairs facing each other, and placed on sheep skins and mats. Over them was an awning of thatch make of palms, which kept the sun off. Four blackies sat in front, two on each side paddling, and four behind, with a man who stood and steered with an oar. It took us forty minutes to paddle down to the mission, and then Father Lutz came and received us. They have a small population of men, women, and little children who have been redeemed from slavery, and some from death, and these are being made Christians. They are among a very fierce savage tribe at Onitsha ; but the people are getting attached to them, and come in numbers to be *doctored*. The chapel is very plain and simple : mud walls whitened, thatched roof, and the floor covered with mats. There are two Fathers and two Brothers. The little children sang hymns with an harmonium, and said prayers during the Mass, and after Mass Father Lutz gave them a very simple talk about the Gospel of the day, which a man interpreted to the natives.

After Mass we sat a bit with the Fathers, and Father Lutz told me how glad he was I had come out—so, Bernard dear, God has allowed me to do the principal work for which I came out. Before I came out, a woman was brought to the mission in chains. She was to be killed or driven away as a *witch*, but the man to whom she belongs as a slave, brought her to the Fathers, and said, if they could get her away, she would be saved. So we arranged that she should be sent up as soon as possible to the mission at Lokojah, and meantime they promised not to kill or injure her. We left in our canoe at ten, and it took a bit over an hour to get back, as the stream was against us. We saw some fine and beautiful birds, large like cranes and ospreys, and some lovely smaller sorts. The heat here is very great and trying, because there is so little breeze, and when there is any from the back it is much cut off by large trees. Father Lutz is coming to us on Thursday, and will say Mass here and give us Holy Communion on Friday, the feast of the Precious Blood. I am keeping very well, and so is Kane, but I wish it was cooler, especially at night. We had a very fine view over the great river on to a large island, over which we cannot see. We know nothing of what is going on in the great world, but mercifully the cable tells me that my dear ones are *serene*. . . . I hope you are able to take good care of the ladies, and it comforts me much to think of what a kind help you are to them in every way you can. How I shall enjoy having some *walks* with you.

Your loving
FATHER.

Asaba, March 23rd to 31st.

For the next mail I am not going to send off hurried letters by each river steamer that happens to come here. Mr. Flint, the Agent General, takes good care of our letters as well as of ourselves, so I shall write quietly on till near the time. There is no homeward steamer due at Akassa now that we can catch until the 8th of April. We are getting on very well altogether; but I feel the heat very much, because there is so little of anything that can be called a breeze. We had some strong Harmattans for a few days, which crumpled up the books and cracked the furniture in style, and I felt refreshed by them. Yesterday afternoon the thermometer inside this cool house was close on 89°, without a breath of air. However much interested I may be and may still get in the work, I can assure you, my dear Allie, that I have neither wish nor intention to remain longer than the *Roquelle*, at the very outside; and I have a very great longing for the day of her leaving Akassa for *home*. I want to go up the river as far as Lokojah, which will give me some variety, and let me more into the working of the Company. I intend to go as soon after Easter as I can get an opportunity.

Kane and I have been a good deal exercised in mind at finding that the natives here carry on the brutalities of killing slaves quite near our house. There is no head king with his chiefs; but there are an immense number of chiefs or headmen, who wear red caps and carry ivory horns, which they blow to let people know they are coming. They also smear their faces with white paint, and have a very revolting look. Throughout the tribe, which is extensive, there are said to be some five hundred of these men, who elect a council of fifty to carry on some sort of government. This want of a head power will, I think, make it easier to break them down if necessary. Every man, before he can wear a red cap, has to kill two slaves; and, when one of them dies, at least three are killed. I was ruminating much about it yesterday, and about what we could do to stop it, when I received a message from the chiefs at Asaba to the effect that they had heard that two great men had come out here, and that they wished to pay them a visit. We sent for the interpreter, who knows the place well, and said I should not see them unless I could talk straight about slave-murder. He said he thought it would be an excellent opportunity for doing so ; and therefore we have arranged to receive them on Tuesday, when I pray God to give me strength and wisdom to let them know that this murder *shall* be put an end to, and that we shall hang every chief or other person convicted of murder.

Our life here as a rule is very monotonous : Rise about six, and have tea, with captain's biscuits and potted meat, fruit, &c. Then I generally do writing, as I am doing now, or letters to the Council, or continue a private book of notes, which I am writing, of all I hear and see for the use of the Council. . . .

Palm Sunday, March 25th.—Kane and I went to Onitsha in a fine new canoe this morning, larger and faster than the other. We all had palms, but there was no procession, and during the long Gospel the *Miserere* was sung, a good way of keeping these poor people from getting weary. We had a chat with the Fathers after it and a cup of chocolate. Fortunately, like last Sunday, the morning was cloudy and felt cool, though on looking at the thermometer before starting, *i.e.*, at 7 a.m., it stood at 79°. Dear Father Lutz spoke so cheerily of the influence our attending Mass has already had. The witch I wrote about has gone off to Lokojah, and her master who brought her to the mission for safety, and is one of the flock of the Protestant mission, has become a catechumen. I was specially glad of the visit to the little mission chapel to-day, as a terrible thing has taken place at Lokojah, which will be very bad for the Company and will throw a heavy responsibility upon me. . . .

On Friday afternoon, the interpreter, Mr. Taylor, took Kane and myself to visit the Juju Grove, where the human sacrifices take place. Two of his men went with us, not a native of this place would dare to have done so. We went by a quiet unfrequented way, having a gun, to look as though we were out for sport, and we got to the place. There is a cleared space, surrounded with huge trees and bush, which gives it a very weird, superstitious appearance, but there were not as many relics of murders as I expected, as they throw the corpses into the bush and animals devour them. But there were two skulls, apparently of children, which had not been carried off; and, please God, next Tuesday I will tell those chiefs something they have never yet heard, and perhaps I may have the comfort of knowing that my visit has struck an effectual blow against these horrors.

We have been on the Niger one month to-day, and I am happy to assure you that all the inducements which led me to forsake you and the little ones have so far been more than fulfilled. We have gone through a time of terrible trial, Allie dear, and my life here makes me long to get away, but I feel that I shall leave a mark here deeper than anything I have yet done, and I hope Kane will have the strength to carry it on, and do an immense deal of good. He keeps quite well, with an unfailing appetite, and he is never up as early as I am. However, he sits up later most nights. By 8.30 I am generally ready to retire for devotions and bed. . . .

Wednesday, 28*th*.—We held the great meeting yesterday, and it passed off so quietly and we think successfully, that I added the code word "Success" and "Peace" to a telegram I have sent down to Brass this morning. I will tell you about it.

In the morning, shortly before breakfast, I felt bilious. The heat of the previous day had, I think, brought it on, and my tongue was *furred*. I could not look at breakfast, but felt quite inclined for rusk and milk, so I lay down and took a bowl of it. Dr. Crosse was about and he wanted me to put off the meeting, but I felt better and anxious for it, and I may say at once, I threw the sickness off altogether, and was *very* hungry for dinner. I kept very quiet whilst our room was being cleared and prepared for the Durbar. Soon there was a constant noise of blowing of horns, tinkling of bells, &c., and the interpreter, Mr. Taylor, came to say that the chiefs had assembled in the market-place and were ready to come. So we put on our robes, and the Commandant came, and one of the officers took my cane. The chiefs came into the compound one after the other with their attendants, all the horns blowing together, making a terrible noise. When they had all been placed we went in with our procession, and sat on three chairs at the end of the room. I, as Chief Justice, in the middle, Kane on my right, Harper on the left, with the staff-bearer alongside. Father Lutz and the Asaba Protestant minister also sat with us by invitation, and Dr. Crosse. There were about forty red-cap chiefs, besides the attendants, so that the room and verandah were crowded. They looked dreadful with the white paint on their faces, and some with eagle's feathers sticking straight out from their ears, and I began to feel my courage about speaking straight out rather diminishing. The Commandant then saluted them, and introduced me as the Great Judge.

I then stood up, and had intended, after the usual salutation, to be excused if I sat down. But I felt so strong, and such increasing determination to speak out, let the

effects be what they might, that I stood all the time.   I
spoke without feeling a bit tired, and was quite prepared
to act energetically if there was a row.   I began by telling
them that I had been a Judge in Africa not far from here
for a long time, sent out by the Great Queen; that I was
a great friend with the chiefs and people, that the chiefs
sat with me in court and held palavers with me, of my
also being at Lagos, where I heard much of the Niger, and
knew many of those who come here for trade, and that I
was good friends with the chiefs and people there.   In
time, I found my health and strength would not allow of
remaining longer, so I went home, and told the Great
Queen I could not go out any more, and sat down in
my home with my family to rest and be quiet.   But that
I kept up great interest in the countries where I had
been, and also in the Niger countries, as I belonged to
the Niger Company.   That it was then found necessary
to send out judges here, and as I had been out so much,
I was asked to go and be the Judge.   I said "No, I am
too old, I cannot; but that I would go for a short time
and take a younger judge who could stay on."   This led
to the crucial part.   I said I came here hoping to be
friends with the chiefs and people, as I had been in the
other countries; but that, when I came, my heart was
made very sad, for I found that all the chiefs were
murderers.

There was a slight movement of uneasiness, but
not a word.   I then went hot at it; told them we
had been to their Juju Grove, and seen the place of
murder, and seen the skulls of two *children* who had
been lately murdered.   I also told them I had received
information that *three* persons had been murdered only
two days ago at another place close by (it was at the
funeral of a chief), and that this would not be allowed,
and that the strongest measures would be taken to put it
down; that I should let it be known among the slaves,
that they might look to us for protection; and that
whenever it was known that a murder was going to
be held, the soldiers would be at once sent, and
that chiefs and Juju-men would be liable to be
hanged; and that I had once sent a chief, his head-

J

man, and Juju-man to be hanged for this very thing. I
told them, when I went back, I should tell the great
chiefs of the Queen what I had seen, and what I had
said to them, and that I knew that, even if the Company
were not strong enough to put it down, the Queen would
send her ships up here if necessary. I finished by saying
it was no subject of palaver, it was a case of peace or
war. They were very uncomfortable, and here and there
some of them tried a contemptuous laugh, especially one
huge creature more ornamented than any of them, who
doubtless greatly enjoys murder. I then returned to the
friendly strain, and hoped all would be peace and friend-
liness, and that my brother-judge would soon be as good
friends with them as I had been with those under me.

I then introduced Kane, who, in a few incisive
words, impressed upon them that when I left there
would be no change whatever in the carrying out
of what I had said. We then retired, to let them consult; but I said they need not at present give a reply to
what I had said about murder. When they were ready
we went in again, and one of them spoke and said the
chiefs saluted and welcomed us, and were glad we did
not ask for an immediate reply about the killing, as
they would consult with themselves and others before
they did so. They thanked us; but, on his saying
more, there were signs of strong dissent among the
others, so, with a few friendly words, the affair came to
an end, and immediately there was a burst of talking
and horn-blowing that made us glad when they were
gone to get a liquor-up at the factory.

So ended that—the first blow which has been attempted
at putting down human sacrifices, though carried on
constantly quite near the barracks and head-quarters.
The Company hitherto has done nothing in it, nor even
to mitigate the worst forms of slave-dealing and slavery.
That goes on under their eyes. Weakly children are
constantly sold to these Asabas cheap, and they do for
sacrifice. I have forgotten to say that, at the finish of
my warning, I said: "You think that the great God,
Who made the white man and the black and all the
world, and Who wished us all to live happily together

here, will keep these slaves you murder to be your slaves in the other world, bah!" I then held up my finger at them and said, "You must all die, and when you die you will see who is right."

Taylor has been in to tell us of the effect, which he says has been very great. He was quite prepared to see them start up and go away in a fury, but only one of them was inclined for that, and the others put him down at once. They were very anxious to know how we got to the Juju Grove, but he evaded it, saying white men go about everywhere. There were slaves present, and Juju-men, and people from far and near, and, he says, when they got together, several at once said that what we had spoken was quite right, so there is a party formed at once to put it down. Taylor seemed to think the effect was great, and that the news would fly in all directions. Both Father Lutz and the minister, a good young fellow from Lagos, were highly pleased, and, if this were the only thing I did, I feel I have not come for nothing.

But imagine my feelings when, just as we were preparing to go in, the mail of the 11th of February arrived! I got out your telegram of the 16th of March, and that made me comfortable for the time.

March 31st.—Poor dear Kane is down with fever, and with a smart attack. Unfortunately, he would not give in at once, and even carried on a preliminary examination of the mutineers with fever upon him. Yesterday (Good Friday) was I hope the worst day, and he certainly had his cross laid on him. But he is going through it all with his usual patience and pluck, and last night he was not very feverish and slept pretty well, so altogether I think he is going on well, and Dr. Crosse has stayed in the house of a night, and been within call all day, so he has had every attention. . . .

We were to have gone to the mission together this afternoon, to spend Easter Day with them, and to enable us to go to Confession and Holy Communion without so much fatigue. But I shall have to go alone now.

I shall begin the trial of the mutineers on Monday. . . . With this and going to Onitsha, I may not have

much more leisure time for writing before the next mail
is made up for Akassa, so I will get my letters into such
form that they may be ready to go off when necessary.
We have had a tremendous tornado and two smaller
ones with deluges of rain, which found its way into this
house in several places. We had to remove Kane with
his bed from where it was. Fortunately I remembered
there were two stoves sent out, and had one burning in
each of our bed-rooms, as the air was reeking with damp.
I am so delighted to think that on this day fortnight the
Roquelle ought to sail to fetch me home. I am very
anxious for *many* reasons to hold on till then, but *no
more.* Short as my stay has been, I do not think I ever
felt a stronger craving to go *home.*

Onitsha, Niger Territories,
April 10th to 21st, 1888.

Yesterday I got a telegram from you which said you
hoped all was at *peace* here. Strange to say, I got it on
board a steamer, to which I and Kane had just been
taken, in order to get us out of the possible reach of the
Asabas, who were besieging our house and the barracks,
and thirsting for our heads. This is all owing to our
determination to put down slave murders, and this is
why I am now writing at Onitsha, listening to the firing
of big guns, which let us know that these savages are
having a lesson. But I had better tell you all about it.

Our last letters went off on Friday the 6th, early in
the morning, and I sent you a telegram " Pluck." After
all the white men who had been present at the trial had
gone away, Mr. Taylor, the political agent, came to tell
us that one of the principal chiefs was to be buried that
evening, and that three slaves were already round the
corpse, and would be murdered at night. Also, that
another chief was dead, and that his funeral would follow.
I felt it was impossible to put up with this, and sent for
Captain Harper, the commandant, who at first spoke of
the whole thing as easy to be done. But when it came
to actual arrangements to march upon the house and
rescue the slaves, he said he would send Gordon with
the men, and remain himself near home to be ready to

do all sorts of things as soon as a shot was fired.   Allie, dear, I remembered I had promised to keep out of fighting ; but when I saw that this man would not go, and would leave it to a new man like Gordon, I felt I must tell him that *I* would go with the men.   He seemed quite pleased, and proposed I should take charge of the Gardner gun, which I declined.   Kane was only recovering from his fever, but declared he would go too. So a strong force was got ready, and, with Mr. Taylor and a band of foreign natives in his employ leading, we marched out of the barracks, Kane and I occupying a place between the two companies of soldiers.   For a time we did not see many people, but they increased as we got on, and we saw many guns (only flint affairs) and horrid spears.   As we got near the place the excitement increased, and some were perfectly frantic, and apparently only restrained from firing by the force of those about them.   Mr. Taylor then told us that the corpse and the slaves had been removed, so we were in a fix.   If one shot was fired, a general fight would begin ; and I seemed almost to hear you begging me to avoid that, and as I knew that I should certainly be the main object of attack, I gave no warlike counsel ; and, at a moment when a collision seemed imminent, I stood behind a huge cotton-tree as a protection.   Fortunately, some of these excited creatures then brought stools and sat down, meaning they wanted to talk ; so I and Kane went up to them, and Mr. Taylor interpreted.   They promised they would not kill the slaves.   I proposed to Mr. Taylor that we should seize one of them as a hostage ; but, fortunately, he thought we were not strong enough, as the warriors were collected in all directions.   So we accepted their promise, and they thanked us for having come to visit them.

I had tried to make some acts of resignation to dying, if necessary, in so good a cause, and to think that my family would be proud at all events of that part of it ; but I felt strongly I would rather not, and that you would rather not also.   So we accepted these terms, and commenced our march back.   The crowds of armed natives on each side let us see that we should have had

a hot time of it, though I dare say our rifles would have
made quick work of them.   But they would have had
lots of shots at us, and slugs out of a flint gun at short
range do damage.   But no one fired, and Mr. Taylor
kept telling the people that the matter was arranged.
At one part, several red-cap chiefs met us, and I
harangued them about it all, and hoped they would be
sensible, and give up killing people; but they only
answered sulkily that it was evident we intended to drive
them out of the country.

Presently we came upon a reserve of our men, ready
to help us to fight our way back; but the fine thing was
that, when we were close at home, another company of
our men suddenly sprang up from behind a bank, giving
me a turn, thinking that we were caught in an ambush.
But we soon saw they were our own men with the commandant, at the end nearest the barracks. So we got
safe back, and I unbosomed my feelings to Kane, as to
what on earth I should say to you, and whether I should
confess by letter or wait till I got home. He thought I
had better take the latter course, and amused me so by
telling me how much he had suffered in mind, as to
what he should say if he had to write and tell you I had
been shot.   His constant anxiety about me is quite
touching.

That same night the three slaves were murdered, and
preparations commenced for the funeral of another chief.
Every one felt that to draw back now would be to give
up everything; and that the Company might at once give
up attempting to govern.

After the murder, large bands of armed men prowled
about our premises and the barracks, thinking we might
march out immediately. Extra guards were put round
our house, and, as I was not told of this, and got up in
the night to wander about, as I often do, to get cool, I
got a decided fright by hearing a noise at the fence, and
seeing in the darkness three men come towards the
house. I prepared to make a rapid movement for the
barracks; but a sentry came up, and on my asking who
they were, he told me it was the guard keeping a look-
out. I then went to bed again, but could not sleep for

the heat, and on going to the door into the verandah, found a man standing close to me. "Who's there?" I shouted, and I could make out that he stood to attention instead of spearing me, so I kept quiet for the rest of the night, and slept well.

On Saturday, the 7th of April, Mr. Taylor came to tell us that the chiefs had sent messengers to talk over the state of affairs, and complained of some trade disputes with the Company. I sent word I had nothing to do with trade palavers, and as word had been broken with me, I would not see them. Afterwards a steamer arrived with Mr. Seago, one of the Company's agents, and he saw them, and found them very defiant, and they said they were quite ready to fight. He did not seem to think much of their threats, and sailed off again. On Sunday we went to the mission in a canoe, and as we came back close under the banks, I felt a little uneasy lest we might be attacked. On landing, Mr. Taylor told us he had received another message, by which he gathered that they did not understand my not seeing the messengers, and were not inclined to give in. No more was I. So I sent word, with regard to the new funeral, that I was not asleep, but had my eyes open. During the afternoon there was a good deal of drumming, horn-blowing, and singing, and I thought it as well to have a few extra men about, as a mere palm-fence was all that separated our grounds from these savages.

After dinner, Captain Harper came over very excited, to say that a message of open war had come. We sent for Mr. Taylor, who was much more subdued than usual, and he told us that the old men had no further power to restrain the young warriors, and that they were determined to fight, but seemed unwilling to attack, and wanted to draw us into the bush. They had been shouting and gesticulating during the day, to make our men fire. They said they wanted to make us fire first. We, on the other hand, wanted to wait till we could get more white men. But Mr. Taylor said they were determined to fight, and that the order had been given that if any man killed a white man, he would not be told of. He said they were gathering all

about the premises, and were most anxious to catch
certain people. I saw he did not come to the point,
so said to him: "Do you mean they want to catch
me?" "Yes, sir," he promptly replied, and that they
wondered I got back the other day. They want to catch
me most, and Kane, and then himself. We then asked
if he thought I should be taken over to the barracks for
the night, and he said he certainly thought so. This
was very unpleasant, but there was no getting out of it
now; and, as a road runs between the judicial and
military compounds, at the end of which the enemy
swarmed, I was taken across with a strong guard round
me. At the request of those left in our house, I asked
for a guard of thirty men, to go over there and protect
them and the premises. Would you believe it? Captain
Harper and Gordon both advised that our house, and
everything in it and all the compound, should be abandoned to these people, and that Kane and all of them
should come into the barracks. None of us non-military
men would hear of it, and the guard was sent. But
what can be done with such men as these, who ought to
have, I think, prevented my running away to the barracks
by forming round the house? The commandant gave
me his bed, which I took, and I lay down feeling far
from happy, but I slept well enough till four, when I got
up to see what was doing. The enemy were said to be
holding a great meeting.

At six I went back to my house to get tea, and to
see how they all were, and found the guard gone, and
only two or three sentries. I sent to request a strong
guard at once, and took my bath and other necessities
with a sentry outside. It was agreed that Kane and I
had much better be removed, as we should require such
constant protection, so we began to pack up. Mr. Taylor
told us he had received a message to say they had
not killed the slaves at the second funeral, but he did
not believe it. Things seemed more peaceable, so we
had our breakfast, and then I had my pipe and a
cup of coffee. All at once there was a great noise
of the Asabas advancing close upon us with their war-
song, so there was a general commotion, and I left my

coffee, but *not* my pipe. I made promptly for the barracks, poor Kane holloaing to beg me to wait till he could collect the guard to go across with me. I knew the guard were busy preparing for the defence, and a capital Houssa sergeant, who was my orderly at Lagos, went with me. I looked up the road, and there they were swarming into the bush just outside the barracks. Kane came with me or after me, and such a scene of confusion I seldom saw, the commandant keeping to the verandah in his pyjamas, and he told me he would stay there and work the gun! I now expected the attack, but the Asabas seemed all to lie down in the bush and keep quiet, and Captain Harper had no anxiety to begin.

Presently the steamer came which was to take us off, and brought a fine Whitworth gun, which was taken up to the barracks. Kane and I were then taken down under a strong guard—quite unnecessary, but it looked well—and went on board, and I certainly felt much safer, and then I got your telegram, hoping I was in *peace*, dated " Brass, April the 5th." So I got it quicker than usual. We sailed to the nearest port where there were white men, and got three to go and help, and then we were landed here, where we live in a rough and most uncomfortable state. We dined at the mission. This morning we were delighted to hear the big guns firing, and there was great excitement here over it. We have had a line to tell about it, and that the commandant let *Dr. Crosse* command a body of men to make a sortie, which had some effect. Dr. Crosse peremptorily forbade us to return yet, so here we are.

I doubt if anything final can be done until Mr. Flint, the Agent-General, returns from Akassa, which I hope will be to-morrow. I know you will scold me for all this ; but I am sure you will forgive me for bringing on a war with these people to put an end to their murdering their slaves. The people here were once bombarded, and seem delighted that the Asabas should catch it. There seldom was a war, great or small, for such a purely good object ; and I want it to be kept up until I get the men who promised not to kill, and then did so, and, if I get them, I hope to hang them in the market-place. You

know how much I advocate kind forbearance with
Africans; but in this case severity only will break
brutality, and I hope it will be carried out to the bitter
end, and until those red-cap chiefs are on their knees
before me. Father Lutz is so pleased that he seems
inclined to go and fight himself. Kane goes with me
heart and soul. The heat is again excessive, even for
this place, and I miss my comfortable bed and chairs.

April 11*th.*—Here we are still, weary and uncomfortable. The news from the seat of war is that they keep
shelling and burning the town occasionally, and preparing
for an advance, but that the *military* officers do not seem
at all anxious for that. I do wish Mr. Flint would come
and push on matters. It is a misery to us being here, in
a house with scarcely any furniture, and nothing to do.
I delight to think that the *Roquelle* will sail next Saturday.
I have neither wish nor intention to stop a day longer
than her arrival on the homeward voyage. . . .

My health keeps all right, though I am very restless
and wakeful at night, and do not eat very much. But I
drink, and some days my chief support is drink—claret
and champagne. I am so thankful I brought a supply
of the latter; but have to give so much to others at
times, that I fear the stock will not last my time. Our
head boy makes capital cock-tails, not strong, and occasionally I take one before dinner with excellent effect.
My own personal servant, Charles, has quite won my
heart. I have told you of my ignominious retreat on
board the steamer. Well, that boy went on packing the
things he thought I would want, without my telling him,
even to pens and ink, and carried everything on board
himself. He even brought the parrot in its cage, and he
seemed quite exhausted in the end. Kane's boy was the
same, but Kane had done more packing than I had
when the panic came. We have heard no firing to-day,
so I suppose nothing is doing. Just heard a big gun
then, so I dare say they are keeping the Asabas awake.

Friday, 13*th.*—Yesterday morning, to our great relief,
a steamer came with a letter to say that, if we wished to
return, it was at our service, and it was evidently wished
that we should go back, if only to try and make Captain

Harper do something. So back we came, and I at once sent for the man, and told him that every one said he was afraid to go out, and that we were being laughed at. He fumed and abused Dr. Crosse, who told him he was a liar, and made him eat his words and apologize; and, in the end, he promised to lead out his men at two o'clock, and did so. Now, I did not go with them, Allie; on the contrary, Kane and I humbly retired on board the steamer until the expedition returned. The noise of firing was tremendous; but I fear it was mostly noise, and that not much has yet been done. However, the enemy have made no signs since, and to-day we are clearing the bush and anxiously waiting for Mr. Flint and others. We slept here in our own beds, and after a bit I slept soundly. First I was disturbed by the firing of our big guns sending shells about the town; then came a tornado, with thunder and heavy rain, and I felt it so cold that I covered myself with a blanket, and was snug till daylight. I sincerely hope you will not hear of this now until I can send you a telegram. When I can explain it all to you, I am sure you will acknowledge that I could not do otherwise than I have done, and I am not going into any of the fighting. My health keeps excellent, and I do not think I look one bit West African. My appetite is not much to speak of, but then I drink, as I think I have already said, and find that as good.

April 14th.—I am very happy to-day at the thought that the *Roquelle* will sail from Liverpool some time to-day. We had a very quiet day yesterday. The enemy made no signs, and our men were kept busy cutting down the bush and trees near our premises; so now they have no shelter, and must come out into the open to attack. I ventured out in the afternoon to inspect the work done, and was much pleased to see a lot of Juju-trees cut down. Some of them were used by the chiefs to dance round after they had killed a man! This may be called a Juju war, so we spoil their groves and images as much as possible; and if I can hang a Juju-man as well as a chief who murdered in spite of me, I shall feel satisfied that we have struck a blow at this devil's stronghold which it will not recover.

I wish you would write a line to Father Scoles, or, of course, see him if you are at home, and tell him I consider the prayers of his community for me have been as fully answered as could well be. Perhaps you could also send a few lines to the Good Shepherd Sisters, Fulham Palace Road, Hammersmith, and tell them all is going on well with me, and that I have never been without the Agnus Dei they sent me. . . .

Afternoon.—One of the chiefs has been down to sue for peace, on the promise they would not kill any more people. I told him, before we talked of peace, they must give up the two men who held the sacrifices, and gave them till Monday morning at daylight to consider it. No one expects they will do this, and that they must have a severe punishment.

Sunday, April 15th.—We could not get to Onitsha for Mass to-day, as our canoe men are all warriors on our side, and also I might be wanted any minute. Things are going better than we expected, and the Asabas are evidently in a wretched state of fear. The chief of the village where the second murderer lives, came in yesterday, and has actually delivered up the man. So we have got one of them, and have made peace with one portion of Asaba. The other part has sent in a strong deputation to-day, including a powerful member of the family of the man we demand—in fact, the man who made the promise to me that the slaves should not be murdered. They said it was very difficult to get the man himself, but seemed to wish we should keep this relation as a hostage, and then it would be more easy to bring in the man himself. In fact, they seem to have brought the man as a messenger like themselves, and then quietly handed him over to us. It strengthens our hands, and I shall not be surprised if the murderer is handed over, though such a thing has never been known on the Niger before. The chief who came in yesterday is the same who came in the Saturday before so defiantly, and the change in the man was most comical. His house has been attacked and looted, and he says he was nearly caught. When brought before me he seemed to shake all over, and the red cap, which they are supposed never to take off, was humbly tucked under his arm. We have been feasting finely here on the bullocks captured, and everybody, boys and all, have had plenty. I have not had such good meat for some time. Altogether, it looks as though it were going to be a great success, not only against human sacrifices, but in establishing the authority and power of the Company, and may be something of a set-off against the Lokojah massacre.

April 18*th*.—To our great relief, the Agent-General, Mr. Flint, arrived on the 16th, and took matters in hand at once. He gave the enemy all yesterday to consider what they would do. In the evening, as we sat at dinner, a message came to say they would not give up the other man we want. We replied at bedtime by sending more shells in various directions. Mr. Flint begged that I and Kane would go on board a steamer, so that they might have no anxieties on our account. So, at five this morning, we got up and went on board the *Kano*, which is armed with a Whitworth gun. Presently the captain took her a little way up a creek, to a spot chosen by himself yesterday, and there administered twenty-four shells in various directions and at various distances. We could not see the town because of rising ground, but the very roar of those shells through the air, finishing with a burst, must have made these savages quake. After this our land force advanced into the town, and did damage to the houses, and actually never saw the enemy. We suppose those twenty-four shells made them fly in all directions. So they all came back safe, and with some more bullocks, which we are glad of, as food was getting scarce, and eight of us sit down at our table daily. I am glad they have destroyed a lot of Juju places, and as a great trophy they brought back the principal Juju image of the whole place, out of the principal shrine of this religion of Satan. So now, I hope, I have done a work which may be much quicker and more effectually done by *force* than by argument. I suspect the visit of the " great man " to the Niger will be remembered for many a day. I hope now I shall soon be able to go to Lokojah. I will try the murderer we

have got, and arrange for his being hanged, and then I
hope I can go. To hang a *chief* for killing a *slave* will
administer a lesson quite unknown in these parts.

April 21st.—I hope there is a chance of this long
letter getting away to-morrow for Akassa. After this
there will be only one mail before the turn of the
Roquelle comes—only one more letter—and then, please
God, I am off for home.

The Asabas are now at our feet, begging for peace,
and even afraid to come in and ask for it. They will
not give trouble again in a hurry. I have as yet only
got the one culprit, whom I will order to be hanged on
Monday morning, and then I will go off to Lokojah.

Asaba, Niger Territories.
Sunday, April 29th, to May 2nd, 1888.

On Monday, the 23rd, I went off in the company's
s.s. *Sockatoo* to Lokojah, and got back again here on
Saturday morning, the 28th. I have cabled both events,
so that I hope you know it is all right. My last letters
were sent off on Sunday last, the 22nd, with the telegram
saying I was going to Lokojah, and putting *pluck* as my
state, and so I considered it to be. However, the strain
upon my mind and body gave way the next morning
after the execution of the murderer; and when I got
on board the *Sockatoo*, I collapsed, and lay down all
day feeling prostrated with weakness. I never hanged
a man on my own authority before; and though I felt
it would be really wrong not to let the sentence be
carried out, and held a formal consultation with Kane
and Mr. Flint, who both took that view, still I was
haunted during the night by the thought I was killing
a man. His hour fixed was six, and when I thought it
was past six, I went to have my tea; but, on happening
to look out, I saw the miserable wretch being taken to
his doom. However, there is no need to write about
this part of the affair; and I am sure I acted rightly,
but, as I said, the strain on my nervous system was such
that it gave way, and I was in a state of collapse. Dr.
Crosse was with us, and was most attentive; and, when
I found relief in a sort of hysterical outburst of crying

and laughing, he told me I must go home in the *Mandingo*, and not wait for the *Roquelle.* Mercifully the day was cloudy and breezy, or it would have been much worse, and I drank champagne, and was better in the evening.

Next day was terribly hot—96° in the saloon on deck, the coolest place, and 122° in the sun. This floored me again, as I did not sleep all night; so that when we arrived at Lokojah early on Wednesday morning, I was not fit for anything but to lie down. The thermometer again registered 96° in the house, some 8° above Asaba; but at five o'clock I managed to walk to the mission, and see the Fathers and Sisters. There was a nice airy room prepared for me, but I knew I should have to talk, and therefore begged to be excused. Dr. Crosse kept beside me, as I walked back easier than I went, as it was cooler. The evening was cool with lovely moonlight, and I bucked up at once, and was quite merry, sitting out with the others after dinner, and some unhappy thoughts as to whether I was sinking passed away. The doctor assured me that pulse and everything was right, so it was only prostration from the heat with short attacks of diarrhœa. On Friday morning, after a fairly good night, I was on board the *Sockatoo* again with the others by 5.30, and away we went for Asaba ; and, though it was as hot as ever, there was such a splendid breeze, it seemed almost like being at sea, and I got better and stronger every hour, and quite enjoyed the scenery up there, which is really beautiful. We went at a rattling pace down the stream, and might have reached Asaba in the evening, but for a temporary breakdown in the engines. So we anchored and came in about eight on Saturday morning, I feeling very well again, and in excellent form. I found Kane very well, and was glad to get back to our house and our own room with its comfortable bed.

At Lokojah I visited the scene of the shooting down of the Sierra Leone men, and became more than ever convinced that it was a horrible massacre. None of the poor creatures who escaped and were "missing" have been found, so I suppose they have died in the bush, or been caught and sold.

We found all quiet here, and after breakfast a festive assembly was held in our house, the main object being to make a presentation of £50 to a popular officer of the constabulary by the executive and medical departments. We gave up possession of the room, and Mr. Flint took the chair, and made the presentation, and then toasts followed. Among those present was Mr. Robinson, a white Church Missionary Society clergyman, who travels about in a steamer, and is a very superior man to any of his sort I have met before. I always enjoy meeting him; and he looks after the black Reverends on the river, who have given so much scandal at times, and made Christianity a by-word and reproach. His health was proposed, and he returned thanks for the Catholics as well, speaking in the warmest terms of them, and he is on most friendly terms with them. Then he proposed my health, and so on it went till we finished a most pleasant gathering, which was also a farewell to Mr. Flint, the Agent-General, who was going off to Akassa to make final preparations for going home by the *Mandingo*, which I hope will also take this.

Fortunately before he left, a thing happened which delighted us all, and which I know will please you too, and make you freely forgive my having brought on a war on behalf of the slaves. Before we separated, Mr. Taylor, the political agent, who has done so much to carry everything through with success, came to me to say that a deputation from the slaves of Asaba had come to thank me and the white men for all we had done for them. So we all sat down, and Mr. Taylor brought in two men, and having pointed to me the poor things bowed down till their foreheads touched the ground. The spokesman said they represented all the slaves of Asaba, and came to thank us for all we had done for them. At first they did not understand it, in fact could not believe that we really made war for them, but now they knew it really was so, and came to thank us. He said they had been hitherto kept like goats and fowls in a yard, and they and their wives and their children taken out to be killed by their masters; but now they knew it would not be so, and they thanked us. I told them it was quite true that we had made the war for them, and if their masters did it again, we should again make war for them. Down went the poor fellows again with their heads to the ground. I pointed to Kane, who sat by me, and said that if ever they were ill-treated they were to come and tell him, and he would look after them, and assured them of protection. The second man, who was older than the speaker, and had not said anything beyond chuckling and making sounds and signs of great pleasure, here stretched out his arms wide, and said something which Mr. Taylor interpreted as, "My heart feels as big as this." We all felt delighted, and that the success of the war was now complete. Mr. Robinson was present, and I only wish Father Lutz had been there too. But we told him of it to-day after Mass, and his face beamed with pleasure. Those slaves have more than rewarded me for having come out. We were all so struck with their superiority in appearance, manners, and talk, to their odious cruel masters, who, thank God, are crushed for the present.

The Company has made a very good thing out of the war, as we not only cut down the bush outside the barracks and judicial compounds, but took possession of the ground also, and so have enlarged the Company's property very much, and made it much safer as well. The Asabas can never again come hiding close up. This is an indemnity for the cost of the war, and will give much more room for future buildings. Were it not for the Lokojah massacre it would be quite a feather in the Company's cap, and I only hope it may act as a set-off against the other. At all events, it is a feather in my cap, and Mr. Flint left us in quite a state of excitement at the success, which he acknowledged the commercial department did not bring about, and he thinks never would, unless I had put my foot down.

The *Roquelle* is due on May 20th, and I do hope nothing more will happen of an exciting character.

The King and chiefs of Onitsha are profoundly impressed, and, through Father Lutz, have begged me to pay them a visit, which I intend to do next week, but that is all friendly. The week after, please God,

K

I shall proceed down the River Niger to Akassa to meet
the *Roquelle*, and most happy and thankful I shall be to
find myself on the voyage *home*.   Dr. Crosse has photo-
graphed this house, and I hope it will turn out well;
but photography is very difficult out here, especially
with the violent sunshine and shades.   He is a very
nice man, and looks after me most tenderly.

May 1st.—Never was a May day more welcome to
me than to-day, and I am unutterably thankful to be
able to say I am going off *this* month.

We have had no letters from home since April 16th,
and are anxiously looking for the next steamer from
Akassa, which may come any day now, but she generally
goes aground.   I believe the Niger is lower this year
than has ever been known.   I shall have a light draft
steamer to take me down.   To miss my steamer by
sticking on a sand-bank would be too dreadful!

And now I make the end of letter-writing, and soon
I trust will be on the ocean again, but *homeward* bound.
May we all have a happy meeting!

It has been thought best to give the account
of these events in the original letters written on
the spot.   We may, however, supplement them
by some extracts from Sir James' narrative in
The Month.   After relating the interview with the
slaves, he continues :

Shortly after this, Mr. Macauley, the minister, came
to tell me that seventeen slaves had been to service at
his church, and wished for instruction. . . . On the
following Sunday, a great many more came to the
mission and factory, including about one hundred and
sixty male and female slaves belonging to the chief
named " Effuni" who was "wanted" for the murder of
slaves at the first funeral.   This man had fled for refuge
to a neighbouring tribe, and sent for his slaves to follow
him there.   The slaves of the Asabas are kept in little
villages by themselves, and do farm and other work for
their masters, and used to be taken out for slaughter

when required. Effuni's slaves declined to follow him,
and came to the factory to inquire if it was really true
that they would be protected. On finding it was so,
they resolved to establish their independence. On
another day I met a deputation of about forty others at
Mr. Macauley's mission, who came to express their
gratitude. In doing so, they said they feared that when
I left they would be killed as usual, but I assured them
that my successor would act just as I had. They then
told me that some of them having come to the mission
had been put in irons for it by their master. On hearing
this, I sent for the chief Obi Raffoo, who acted as
negotiator between the Company and the Asabas, and
told him to let it be known that, though I did not wish
for any more punishing, yet that if they used irons in
this way, I would put them in irons. This had an
immediate effect, and I heard of no more trouble on that
score:[1]

The opportunity for establishing a Catholic
mission at Asaba opened up by these events,
brings out the points that Sir James Marshall
had always insisted upon. It seems that there
was a mission at Lokojah, situated at the con-
fluence of the Binué with the Niger. This lies
within the Mahommedan country of Nupé, where
there is, as Sir James says, "about as much chance
of making converts as in Cairo." Yet the Society
of African Missions passed over the three hundred
miles of country full of heathen, and sent missionaries to Lokojah, where he found "three Fathers
and three Sisters with very little to do. They
had redeemed a few children, whom they were
educating. . . . Two more Fathers had, in accordance with orders from Lyons, been sent to a

[1] *Missionary Crusade in Africa*, p. 22.

station up the River Binué, where they were not more fully occupied." Sir James continues :

I found two splendid men at Lokojah, Father Poirier, the Superior, whom I had formerly known at Lagos, and Father Zappa, an Italian, who is a man of science as well as theology. . . . I told them what had happened at Asaba, and what an opening there was for missionary work if taken in hand at once. They would have been only too happy and thankful to have moved their whole establishment, together with the two Fathers who were wasting their lives at the Binué station, but questions of jurisdiction placed difficulties in the way. The country on the right bank is in the vicariate of Lagos, and there is no Bishop whatever to appeal to for the arrangement of these matters. The want of a Bishop is another of the many difficulties thrown in the way of these missions. A Bishop living in the country would have been able to prevent many unfortunate occurrences which resulted from their being governed from a distance.

Having talked the matter over, Father Poirier promised that he would go to Asaba at once and see for himself the state of affairs. He followed me there in a few days, and saw that it would never do to lose such a great opportunity, and that he must act at once, and ask for permission afterwards. Father Lutz warmly supported him in this view. We all knew that Father Chausse, the Superior at Lagos, would approve of this course, and soon afterwards, on my way home, I had the satisfaction of seeing him and telling him about it, and receiving from him the most cordial expressions of approval and gratitude for all that had been done. I should think that a similar approval, with further assistance, has now been sent from Lyons, but until there is a Bishop at the head of the clergy and missions in those parts, there must be constant difficulties in the way of organization and development.[1]

[1] Op. cit. pp. 25, 26.

Father Poirier lost no time in selecting a suitable piece of ground, and Mr. Taylor, the political agent, managed the purchase of it from the natives. Lieutenant Gordon started a subscription among the Company's servants, and before Sir James left for England he had the consolation of putting Father Zappa in possession of the new Mission of St. Joseph of Asaba. After his return to England, he received encouraging accounts from Mr. Kane of the new mission, and a letter from Father Poirier, of which the following is a translation :

St. Joseph of Asaba,
July 6th, 1888.

MY DEAR SIR JAMES,—The station of St. Joseph, of which you are the first founder, has raised our greatest hopes. On the 7th of June I arrived at Asaba, and found Father Zappa already installed in the mission. The bamboo house was still incomplete, but little by little it has been finished, and other buildings are rising by its side, so that we have the commencement of a little village. Our house has two rooms, the one for us and the other for the children, and there is a chapel which can hold about one hundred and fifty persons when packed like herrings. After the first Sunday about one hundred and fifty people have come at different times to visit it. Since then the number has gone on increasing. The people listen willingly and with the greatest attention. They repeat with respect the prayers which are interpreted to them, and it seems as though they must profit by them. Last Sunday, after we had instructed them in the Sacrament of Baptism, we baptized two little girls before them. They listened most attentively, and when I asked them if they themselves wished to receive this sacrament which opens the gate of Heaven, they all replied that it was their greatest desire. I feel sure that the good God will bless these good dispositions.

There is one thing which makes us popular, and
which will produce excellent results, which is the practice
of medicine. From the first Father Zappa has been
busy at this work. The sick arrive in numbers, and
before long almost every kind of human malady will
have presented itself before our doctor. We have also
paid visits to the houses of the sick, and have baptized
several in their dying moments. A deaf mute having
learnt by signs that there is only one God, immediaty
consigned his "jujus" to his ancestors. During the last
two days two new-born infants whose mothers had died
were brought to the mission. Fortunately Providence also
sent us a female slave who had fled from Onitsha with
her child, and we received her, feeling sure she would
be of great assistance to us. To-day she has nursed
these three infants, and if her master comes to reclaim
her, I do not know how we shall be able to rear these
two little beings. For in this country no woman likes
to nurse a child whose mother died at its birth, and if
we had not received these two little boys, who are only
eight days old, they would have died. They will be
baptized next Sunday. A short time after you left,
Father Zappa attended a man who was condemned to
death for murder. He was in excellent dispositions,
and at his own request he was baptized before he
died.

Our work among the soldiers has not been without
fruit. Besides the few Catholics who come to Holy
Mass on Sundays, we have also several catechumens
both heathen and Protestant. What we want much is
to get some small books of instruction, and I hope you
will be able to carry out your intention of sending us
some of the little tracts of the Catholic Truth Society.
Mr. Kane and the officers are most kindly disposed
towards us.

In November we will build our permanent house,
perhaps we shall also build one for the Sisters, whom
I intend to ask for as soon as possible. But what an
expense! Truly I do not know how we shall carry on.
Here we already have to support five boys, three women,
two little girls, and three babies. But God watches

over us, and good people who are numerous will come
to our aid.

We are in great want of remedies and comforts for
the sick.

Sir James returned home in June in good spirits,
and with renewed zeal in the cause of African
Missions. But, notwithstanding all the care that
his devoted successor, Mr. Kane, had taken to
spare him fatigue, and assist him lovingly when
ill, it is to be feared that his constitution was still
further weakened by his expedition. He never
expressed the slightest regret at having undertaken
the work ; and, if his life was thereby shortened,
he rejoiced to make the sacrifice in so good a
cause.

CHAPTER VI.

WORK IN ENGLAND. VISIT TO ROME. PLEADS
THE CAUSE OF AFRICAN MISSIONS AT PROPA-
GANDA. AUDIENCE OF THE HOLY FATHER:
THE SLAVERY QUESTION. SUDDEN ILLNESS.
DEATH AND FUNERAL.

WHEN Sir James Marshall returned to England
he found the minds of Englishmen quite alive to
the importance of Africa, and of our possessions
there. The question of slavery was also beginning
to take hold of the public mind. The Jubilee of
Pope Leo XIII. was calling forth a marvellous
expression of loyalty from all parts of Christendom, and the Pope's magnificent letter to the
Bishops of Brazil proclaimed the extinction of
slavery in every Christian State throughout the
world. All this prepared the way for Cardinal
Lavigerie's noble effort to rouse the spirit of
Christian nations to resolve to put an end to
slavery in Africa. Although warmly sympathizing
with the Cardinal's object, it will be seen from the
preceding pages that the subject of this memoir
held different views from the Archbishop of
Carthage as to the best means of effecting that
end. He was, however, extremely glad to observe
the enthusiasm that was excited, and both by

speeches and letters endeavoured to help forward the movement, in hopes that events would prove the truths that he had for so many years been urging on the English, and especially on the English Catholic public. In the autumn of 1888 he prepared for *The Month* three papers on the work which had been done on the Niger. These were published afterwards in a separate form by the Catholic Truth Society, under the title of *The Missionary Crusade in Africa*. In December he attended a great Anti-Slavery Meeting held in Manchester under the auspices of the Geographical Society, at which the Bishop of Salford took a leading part, and read a message of approval and blessing from the Pope, and a letter of sympathy from Cardinal Lavigerie. Sir James proposed the vote of thanks to Mr. Scott, whose paper formed the matter for discussion.

Soon after this he set off with Lady Marshall on a long projected visit to Rome. Writing about the Catholic Truth Conference, he says :

Bishop Vaughan (of Salford) was *very* cordial with me and my endeavours to help on the missions in Africa. At the Conference yesterday he dubbed me the missionary as well as the treasurer of the Society. I have no doubt he will help me much to obtain audience with some of the Propaganda folk. But I am going to try and see the Pope himself about it, especially about giving the missions a Bishop. . . . I want to tell the Pope himself about it, and that will be a grand finish to the work which I have, I believe, been made use of by Almighty God to do, or rather to cause to be done by others.

It will be seen that his main object in going to Rome was to do something for the West African

Missions, and he succeeded beyond his expectations. He had letters to Mgr. Stonor, who took up the cause warmly; and the late Captain Cooper, R.N., introduced him to the Rector of the American College. He writes himself:

I pushed my missions with great vigour and success in Rome. Mgr. Stonor got me interviews with Mgr. Jacobini and Cardinal Simeoni at the Propaganda. I had previously found enthusiastic friends at the American College in the Rector, Mgr. O'Donnell, and Bishop Keane, Rector of the American University. They told me to "wire in" at the Propaganda, and so I did, and put it down in writing as well. Mgr. Jacobini listened most attentively, and I gave him a new map of the Niger country, so that I think they may grasp where West Africa lies. Father Cardella was also most kind and sympathetic, and urged me to tell *everything* at the Propaganda, and to be sure to put it all down on paper. On leaving, the Americans told me I must not rest until the matter is carried out by the appointment of a British subject as Bishop at Lagos, and that I must make the English Bishops take it up, and tell them it will be a shame and a disgrace to them if they do not do so. . .
I do not know what more I can do. I have written to the Bishop of Salford to report progress, and will call on Cardinal Manning—but their hands are very full.
Our visit finished up with a most charming audience of the Holy Father. I was not at all prepared for the loving, affectionate, and fatherly way in which he treated us.

He gives a full account of it in a letter to his little boy:

Hotel Minerva, Rome, Jan. 20th, 1889.
MY DEAR BERNARD,—This day last year was a very sad one in our family, for it was on it that I bid you and mother good-bye at Euston and went off to Liverpool, to set sail next day for the Niger. I left our little Mary

happy and merry, but with her head and leg bandaged up, under Mr. Godler's care in Devonshire Place. I went because I believed it to be my duty to go, and also in the firm belief that it would all end happily and bring blessings upon us.

All this has proved true, and on this very day we have received a most full and loving blessing and benediction from the Pope himself. What a change it is from this day last year. I will do my best to let you know all about it. Last evening I received notice that the Pope would give us an audience to-day at twelve o'clock. This morning we went quietly to a Low Mass at the church close by, and then kept quiet in our room and got ourselves properly dressed in good time. We then drove to the Vatican, and into the courtyard where the entrance to the Pope's residence is. We walked slowly up a very fine marble staircase, every now and then coming upon one of the Swiss Guards in full uniform. It was a long way up, and mother stopped every now and then to take breath. At last we came to the landing of the Pope's rooms. We passed through a fine room into a beautiful large hall, which is occupied by the officers and men of the Swiss Guard on duty. We passed through this into other rooms, until we came to one in which were several men-servants in very handsome scarlet livery. They all bowed to us, for you must remember that an audience with the Pope like ours is a very great honour. When he gives an audience in an ordinary way, he receives a lot altogether; but this was given to our two selves. We then were passed through another room or two until we came to one the walls of which were covered with beautiful tapestry, and chairs were all round the room. Between the two windows there was a table with a very fine large crucifix upon it, the figure of our Lord being in ivory. Here we were asked to sit down, and in the next room we saw two of the Pope's Noble Guard, so we knew we were close to the Pope's room. One of the chamberlains came and told us that the Holy Father was then engaged in giving an audience. We were not sorry to sit and collect our nerves a bit. Presently a foreign Ambassador in full uniform, and his family, passed through, so we thought our turn was coming on. In a very short time the chamberlain summoned us, and we passed through the room where the Noble Guards were, and saw the Monsignor who introduces people standing at an open door waiting for us. We passed in, and were in the presence of Pope Leo XIII.

It was a smaller room than the others, and narrow, and he sat upon a chair raised a little above the ground, wearing a white cassock. We genuflected, and then walked towards him. The rule is to genuflect again before kneeling before him, but his arms were held out towards us, and I do not think we did that part, but went on and knelt down and at once kissed his ring, taking hold of his hand.

The Monsignor said we would talk in French, and then we were left entirely alone with him. He looked at me and said, "So I hear you have been for twelve years out in Africa," and spoke of his great interest in that country at present. I told him that mother had been out also three times, and he was so pleased, and took her hand and held it most of the time we were there. I wish we could have taken down all he said, but we all three talked away, and I told him I could not manage much French, and that mother must do the talking. We told him I had been to the Propaganda, to tell them about West Africa and the missions, and he said he was glad, as they wished to gain all the information they could about Africa.

He also asked what family we had, and mother said, Two. He did not suppose an old fellow like me had such young children as you and Mary, so he asked, What is their career? meaning, what do they do in life. Are they in the army? So mother explained that you are quite young; and what do you think she did next? She brought out a photograph of each of you, and the Pope took them in his hands and patted them, and said, *Quels gracieux enfants!* and gave you both a very loving blessing. Mother then asked him to bless some rosaries, &c., which she had in her handbag. The dear man was not content with merely passing a blessing over them, which is sufficient, but put his hand in all among them, and asked us to give them to our friends and tell them the Pope had touched and blessed them. We asked him for a special blessing on the missionaries in West Africa, which he gave fervently, and bid me tell them from him that he had done so. I also got a special blessing for Mr. Kane. Among other things, he asked how we stood the African climate; and when mother told him I had suffered a good deal, he asked whether I had come to Rome for my health. On which mother said, No ; but that we had come to see him.

I cannot tell you how kind and affectionate he was, blessing us occasionally and putting his hand on our heads. He even asked us to sit down, instead of kneeling before him, but we greatly preferred remaining as we were. He then gave us and our family a most fervent benediction, and we again kissed his ring, and then did the proper reverence to St. Peter and our Lord by kissing his foot, and came away more happy than I can tell.

We passed by Noble Guards and Swiss Guards bowing and saluting, and it seemed like a dream to have had such an interview with the successor of the great Apostle to whom Jesus said, " Thou art Peter, and on this rock I will build My Church," and who, though robbed of the rights conferred upon him by Christendom and unable to move outside the Vatican because of the wicked power which occupies his city, is yet by far the most powerful ruler of the world.

I am sure you will both be pleased to hear about this, and that the Pope saw your photographs and sent you his blessing.

And now, having had this audience, we will prepare to go away. We must pay a good many good-bye visits and pack up, but I hope we may get to Florence on Wednesday.

We should like to hear from somebody when at Venice, and there will be time if it is sent off at once, not later than Friday, so that we may be sure to know your plans. Our address will be—Grand Hotel, Venice. We shall be so glad to see you both again. I feel quite anxious to get home again. Give our love to Aunt Libby and everybody, and please send this letter on to Aunt Hennie to read.

Your loving

FATHER.

Jan. 21st.—This is the day I sailed for Africa.

Sir James Marshall returned home early in February, 1889, and resumed his usual occupations, and his diligent attendance at the Council of the Catholic Truth Society. In April we find him again addressing the readers of the *Tablet* on the subject of African Slavery. He recapitulates the facts that he had been insisting upon ever since 1874, and concludes:

> It is facts like these which I have from time to time proclaimed in the *Tablet* and elsewhere, and which I hope are at last being realized. We have plenty of work cut out for us at our own doors and in our own house, without getting up a cry for fighting expeditions against the Arab slavers. The negro everywhere is as keen a slaver as the Arab, and the white man will never put down slavery by his rifle and sword. For myself, and my African experience is now pretty long, I have no belief in any mode of really reaching the intellect and heart of the African negro, except through and by the missions of the Catholic Church. That is the true crusade for us to work for, and not any crusade of fighting and force which invariably leave matters worse than they were.[1]

On the 11th of June he received through Archbishop Stonor a Brief, by which the Holy Father created him a Knight Commander of St. Gregory, in recognition of his services to the cause of Catholic Missions on the Niger and in West

---

[1] *Tablet*, April 8, 1889.

Africa.   He valued this honour even more than
the honours bestowed upon him by the Queen,
especially because it seemed to him a token that
his efforts in behalf of those missions were on the
point of being crowned with success.

The following is the text of the Holy Father's
Brief:

DILECTO FILIO JACOBO MARSHALL

LEO XIII.

Dilecte Fili salutem et Apostolicam Benedictionem.

Integritas vitæ religionis obsequium factis probatum,
antiqua Romanum erga Pontificem observantia, et quæ
præclara potissimum tui erga rem Catholicam studii
argumenta exhibuisti, quo tempore gubernatoris munere
in provincia "Niger" appellata occiduæ Africæ functus
es, Nobis suadent, ut amplissimum tibi honoris titulum
exhibeamus, qui et meritis tuis respondeat, et propensam
erga te voluntatem Nostram testetur.   Quare te a quibus-
vis excommunicationis et interdicti, aliisque ecclesiasticis
sententiis, censuris et pœnis, quavis modo vel quavis de
causa latis, si quas forte incurreris hujus tantum rei
gratia absolventes et absolutum fore censentes, hisce
Litteris Equitem Commendatorem Ordinis S. Gregorii
Magni classis civilis eligimus, facimus, teque in ornatis-
simum eumdem Equitum cœtum adsciscimus.   Proinde
tibi, dilecte fili, concedimus, ut propriam Equitum hujus
Ordinis et gradus vestem induere ac proprium item
insigne gestare queas, nempe majoris moduli Crucem
auream octogonam rubra superficie imaginem S. Gregorii
Magni in medio referentem, quæ tænia serica rubra,
extremis oris flava collo circumducta dependeat.   Ne
quod vero discrimen tam in veste quam in Cruce hujus-
modi gestandis contingat, appositum schema tibi tradi
jussimus.

Datum Romæ apud Sanctum Petrum sub Annulo
Piscatoris die xxviii. Maii, MDCCCLXXXIX.   Pontifi-
catus Nostri Anno Decimosecundo.

M. CARD. LEDOCHOWSKI.

Loco + Sigilli.

In July, he and Lady Marshall went to Birmingham for the Latin Play at the Oratory. He was always a great favourite there, and used to enjoy mixing with the boys, and his hearty laugh could be heard in the centre of the merriest groups. This time, however, it was noticed that he kept rather aloof from the boys, and was exceptionally grave. He had a good deal of conversation with Cardinal Newman, who took a lively interest in all that he had to say about the West African Missions, and wished the Oratory School past and present to take the matter up. His Eminence was particularly interested in the establishment of a bishopric for the Gold Coast, and subsequently sent Sir James £100 as the commencement of a fund for the benefit of the future Bishop. But no one had the slightest suspicion that the end was so near. Sir James had frequently remarked since the beginning of the year, that it was his fifty-ninth year, and that his father had died in his fifty-ninth year, and he did not think he should live to see the end of the year. Still, his health did not seem to portend any sudden collapse.

On Thursday, the 1st of August, the whole family went to Margate for a change, as it was thought the sea-breezes would benefit little Mary. On Sunday, the 4th of August, he wrote several letters, and among them one to the present writer, in his usual spirits. On the evening of that day, he stayed out rather late on the beach with his children, and at night complained of feeling unwell. It was considered an attack of African fever, and was treated accordingly. The ailment did not, however, yield to the treatment, and on Wednesday the priest, Father Sigebert Sanders, O.S.B., was called in, and also a medical man, who found him suffering from an attack of pneumonia. Sir James saw by the doctor's face that he thought the case serious, and asked, "Am I going to die?" The following letter from Father Sigebert will be the best and most authentic account of the closing scene :

In answer to your inquiry, I may say that the death-bed of Sir James Marshall was one of those scenes that remains indelibly on the memory of a priest, accustomed to assist at many a departure from this world. I do not remember ever passing the house where this occurred without recalling the incidents in prayer.

The whole thing was sudden as to time, but his admirable calm and complete resignation took away all signs of hurry or dismay. The end came on Friday afternoon, and it was only on the Wednesday that we knew the worst. The doctors spoke hopefully in his presence, but we had good reason to believe that the end had come. I then told him that I had the Viaticum with me, and that he had better receive the last sacraments. Without a moment's hesitation, the medical man was told to wait elsewhere, and Sir James expressed the greatest wish to go to Holy Communion, and to be anointed. One thing only he stipulated for, and that was, that all his family should be present. His beloved boy Bernard had to be sought where he had gone to walk with his companions, and although this took some time, he seemed so anxious to impress his son with the solemnity of the event, that we could only silently wait.

He made his General Confession as though he had made an immediate preparation with the greatest care ; and then, saying the *Confiteor* himself, the Sacraments and Last Blessing were given. There was one burning word of farewell for each of his loved ones at that solemn moment ; but no repining, no excessive grief—with perfect control all was subdued, and kept sub-

L

servient to the deepest religious demeanour. One
instruction to the boy to "take care of mother," and
many other little touching incidents took away all inclina-
tion to say many words, but made the hearts swell, and
the tears well up, in all that little group by his side.

On Friday morning I again administered the Holy
Viaticum, and in alternate verses we said the *Anima
Christi* together. His joy in answering the interroga-
tories of the *Ordo* concerning his faith was most edifying.
With something more than a smile, and with the greatest
fervour he replied, and seemed to glory in the fact,
that he was a son of Holy Church. And that he was
being rewarded for his fidelity, I felt most deeply.

But in true Catholic feeling, at such a trial, I did
not know whether to admire more the dying or the
living. Only such a husband and father could have
brought about such surroundings.

Though the time was so short he seemed to
think of everything, and gave minute directions
how his body was to be disposed of, so as to give
the least possible trouble to the landlady. He
retained perfect consciousness to the last, and
kissed the crucifix the Pope had blessed for his
death when no longer able to speak.

A telegram, that had arrived just before his
death, but was not opened until all was over,
contained the blessing of the venerable Cardinal
Newman. Most kind letters from Cardinal
Manning, and numerous other friends, testified
to the esteem and love in which he had been held,
and the deep sympathy that was felt for his widow
in her sudden bereavement.

His remains were brought home to Roehampton
as soon as possible, and on Wednesday, August
the 14th, a Solemn Requiem was sung for the
repose of his soul by Father Scoles, S.J., the

novices at Manresa forming the choir. His eldest brother was present, Dr. Marshall being abroad ; Lady Marshall's sister, and brother-in-law, Messrs. Pope, Bellasis, Allequen, La Serre, and many other Edgbaston friends were there, besides Father Kirk, Superior of the Oblates of St. Charles, and many from London. At the conclusion of the Mass, Canon Brownlow preached from the text :

"Whatsoever thy hand is able to do, do it earnestly; for neither work, nor reason, nor wisdom, nor knowledge, shall be in hell, whither thou art hastening" (Eccles. ix. 10).

Reverend Fathers and dear Brethren.—We are met together to-day on an occasion which is one of great sorrow to all of us. We are met to do the last offices of Christian charity towards one who is very much beloved and whose loss will be very widely felt. He is a loss to us as Englishmen, for he fulfilled his duty well and bravely towards his Queen and country, and the services that he rendered were recognized by the honours which were conferred upon him. He is a loss to the Church of God at large, especially to those foreign missions on the West Coast of Africa, which he had so much at heart. He is a loss to you, the Fathers of the Society and of this place, because he was a good, loyal, and faithful Catholic, and supported your teaching, not only as far as he could by his means, but still more by his noble example. I cannot trust myself to say what a loss he is to those who were near to him—his own family, to every branch of it. You know—those of his relations who are here—how he did his duty to you, and how faithful he was in all the relations of domestic life. There are those here to whom he is a great loss by reason of the warm friendship they entertained for him for many years. He was a most loveable character—one whom no one could know without loving, and those who knew him best loved him most. Many of us here understand and sympathize with the touching lament of the Royal Psalmist for the friend of his youth : "I grieve for thee,

my brother Jonathan, exceeding beautiful, and amiable
to me above the love of woman." But let us turn away,
dear brethren, from our own private feelings, and let us
consider the noble lesson taught us by him who now lies
lifeless and cold and speechless, and yet who speaketh
still.

I thought, when it was entrusted to me to say something to you this morning, before his body is committed to the grave, that no words could express better
the mainspring of his life than those words I have taken
for my text : "Whatever thy hand is able to do, do it
earnestly." I shall divide what I have to say about the
lesson of his life into three parts : First, his earnestness
and in seeking and finding the true faith ; secondly, his
life as a Catholic layman ; thirdly, his life as a Christian.

1. He began his life—at least he began his manhood—
under difficulties. He lost at a very early age his right
arm, and this, which would be to most young men an
entire discouragement, cut him off from that which he
had longed for from his youth—to be a soldier, to serve
his country in India. Still, he felt that he must make
up his mind to do the best he could under the circumstances, and you know how wonderfully he made that
one left arm of his do a great deal more than both arms
of most men do. Afterwards, he found himself led by
circumstances to devote himself to what he then considered the service of God in the Protestant ministry.
I suppose it will be a surprise to some of his friends
to hear that Sir James Marshall was ever an Anglican
clergyman. He never liked to speak about it, because
he always felt that he had been to a certain extent in a
false position, and it was difficult to explain ; but I don't
think you can form an adequate idea of the difficulties
he had to contend with unless you take that into consideration. I am not going to say, however, that even
in this position he did not fully carry out the words of
my text : "Whatsoever thy hand is able to do, do it
earnestly." For, when he devoted himself to the ministry
in the Anglican Church, he did it with all his heart and
soul ; and he tore himself away from his first curacy in
the country to come to London, to be, as he expressed

it at the time, "chained to the Cross," that he might work and labour for the good of souls in the thickest population and one of the poorest districts of this vast metropolis. He devoted himself to working among the costermongers and other poor people who throng the courts and alleys in the parish of St. Giles, Cripplegate. There he used to preach in the open courts and visit constantly the poor people; and he did really a good and lasting work, as is shown by the number of those to whom he ministered who afterwards followed him into the Catholic Church, while many who did not have that blessing remember with gratitude, even at the present day, what he did for them.

Then, at last, there came upon him—that which comes upon so many earnest Anglican clergymen— there came the revelation of the true Church of God. It burst upon him rather suddenly, and filled him with great anxiety and trouble. It seemed to him at the time like giving up everything to which he had devoted his heart and soul. He had to give up his work, and the loss of his arm prevented his ever having the hope of being a Catholic priest. You must take these things into consideration in order to form an idea of what a sacrifice it was to him. I was in constant communication with him at the time, and I knew well how that affectionate, sensitive heart of his bled at the extent of the trial he went through. I remember how, shortly before he was received into the Church, by prayer and study all his doubts disappeared. They vanished away, and in their place came a full and consoling certainty of the firmness of the rock on which the Church was built. He was a man, not of great profundity in study, nor, perhaps, of great profundity in thought, but he was a man who was able, by a certain true instinct he had, to seize upon the main points of books he read and of the subject to which he gave his attention. Therefore, he did not set himself to clear up all those minor points of detail, with which so many Protestants, who are drawn towards the Catholic Church occupy themselves. He set himself at once to the main point: Has the great Divine Head of the Church left any

distinct indication of His will as to how His Church is
to be kept?[1]   And when he remembered the words,
"Thou art Peter, and upon this rock I will build My
Church, and the gates of Hell shall not prevail against it,"
his earnest heart asked whether those words, as understood by Catholic tradition, involved what the Catholic
Church teaches to-day.   Then, when all doubts were
cleared away, he turned to the Church with the simplicity
of a little child.   He wrote to me a few days before his
reception, and said : "All my doubts are vanishing
away, and are replaced by certainty.   I shall knock at
the gate boldly, and the gate will be opened to me, and
I will go in and be safe with Jesus and Mary and the
angels and saints in the bosom of God."   And from that
day to the moment of his death never one misgiving,
never one doubt as to what he had done crossed his
mind.

2. Next, after his reception into the Church, which
you will have seen was the effect of his doing earnestly
what he had to do, he exemplified those words still more
by his life as a Catholic.   You know that the position of
a convert to the Catholic Church who has been an
Anglican minister is one always of great difficulty.   He
descends at once from the chair of teaching to the floor
of discipleship.   He must forget that he has ever been
anything like a teacher, and he must submit himself with
the simplicity of a child and ask to be taught.   And
then, too—unless he has a vocation for the priesthood,
where his course is very simple and clear—he very often
has great difficulties from a temporal point of view.
He has no means, perhaps, of subsistence, and has to
seek a livelihood by occupations for which his previous
life has utterly unfitted him, and which are often very
uncongenial to him.   Our departed friend felt all this,
and felt it deeply, but he bravely and earnestly took
in hand what had to be done.   He did not sit still
groaning and complaining over his lot, but set at once to
work to see how he could love and serve God in the new
position in which God had placed him.   He was for
some time at St. Mary's, Bayswater, where his musical

[1] See p. 2, note.

talents and powers of organization made him of great use to the Fathers. Then he devoted himself to tuition, and some of the happiest years of his life were spent at the Oratory School of Cardinal Newman at Birmingham. And never has he lost the place he gained in the great Cardinal's kind, affectionate heart, and never will he be forgotten by the masters and pupils of that school.

Then, by the advice of a friend whose judgment he greatly relied upon (Mr. Serjeant Bellasis), he resolved to devote himself to the study of the law; and taking advantage of the Act of Parliament which enabled him then to be called to the Bar, he became a barrister. In due course of time he was offered the appointment of Chief Magistrate on the Gold Coast, and that was his career in the latter part of his life. He rose from being Chief Magistrate to be first puisne Judge and then Chief Justice of the Gold Coast. And, before he had been in the colony six months, he was called upon to assist Sir Garnet Wolseley and the troops in the Ashanti War, his services on that occasion being recognized by the medal he received. All this time he set an example of steady perseverance and resolute courage in the midst of trying circumstances. It would be impossible for me now to occupy your time by telling you of those trying circumstances. The climate was one; the isolation another; the absence for many months at a time from the possibility of hearing Mass or going to confession was another. All these difficulties were in his way, and yet, by the grace of God, he overcame them all.

3. The third point I wish to call your attention to was his earnestness in the service of God. He did not go out to West Africa simply and solely to make a fortune. He had the idea in his mind, when he first went out, to be a help and consolation to those devoted priests who are giving themselves up to the work of saving souls in that deadly climate. When he got there he obtained the affection and confidence of the natives, and he used that affection and confidence, as far as he possibly could, in leading them to the true faith, and in giving them, as far as he was able, the blessing of Christian civilization. And then, as time went on, and as his influence

increased, he was still more able to do what he had then taken in hand, and to do it earnestly. You know very well, many of you, how earnestly he wrote and wearied many of his friends by his importunities, in season and out of season, that we in England should take an interest in those poor benighted populations—those heathen populations which form part of our own dominions, and towards which we, as Englishmen, owe a special duty, and, as Catholics, a more particular duty. Thus he laboured, in season and out of season, for the good of the souls by whom he was surrounded. His work was happily crowned by a partial measure of success even before he died. He was able to visit Rome and have an audience with the Holy Father; and he pleaded their cause with the Holy Father and the authorities at Rome, and obtained a more satisfactory and permanent basis for the missionary establishments on the West Coast. In recognition of his services to the cause of the Catholic missions, the Holy Father bestowed upon him that Order which he valued even more than those bestowed on him by his Queen—the Order of the Knight Commander of St. Gregory. Well, now you see that in relation to the three points—his life before he became a Catholic, his generosity in embracing the faith at the risk of all the sacrifices it involved, and his steady perseverance in duty—he did the work which came before him, whatever it might be, with all his heart and soul. In these different ways you see he set us all, priests and people alike, an example and illustration of the text: "Whatsoever thy hand is able to do, do it earnestly."

Yes, dear brethren, but "What shall it profit a man if he gain the whole world and lose his own soul?" The care of his own soul was a point which our departed friend never once lost sight of. He had for many, many years a tender filial devotion to the Blessed Mother of God. He always considered that he owed his conversion especially to her patronage and intercession. He never failed in his devotion to her wherever he might be, either here or in those far distant lands; and she was with him when he came to die, and she obtained for him the blessing of one of the most happy and consoling deaths I have ever heard of. The priest who had the privilege of attending him on his death-bed thanked God for the privilege of seeing so thoroughly Christian and Catholic a death. He received the summons of his death with no perturbation, no anxiety. It seemed as though he had been expecting it and waiting for it, and when it came it was only as if a guest was suddenly announced to him. He at once desired that he might receive the last sacraments of the Church; and, as he lingered one day beyond the day on which he received them, by his earnest request he received the Holy Viaticum over again before receiving the Last Blessing. Up to the very last he maintained consciousness, and he gave directions for those left behind in order to save them trouble and anxiety. So he departed to his God, and so he fulfilled those words which he had used on his reception into the Church: "I shall knock boldly at the gate, and the gate will be opened to me, and I will go in and be safe with Jesus and Mary and the angels and saints in the bosom of God." Yes, may the angels conduct thee to Paradise; may the martyrs greet thee on thy coming; may He Who died for thee receive thee! And let us, dear brethren, who remain behind gather up the lessons which his noble self-denying life has left us. From his disinterested example we may learn to have strength in difficulties, and to remember that "Whatsoever thy hand is able to do, do it earnestly."

But there is one part of my text which does not apply to him. It is true that in the days of King Solomon the dead went to that part of Hell called Limbo, and then it might truly be said, "There is neither work, nor reason, nor wisdom, nor knowledge in hell, whither thou art hastening." But this is not true now. Jesus Christ has descended into Hell, and has made that Hell Paradise. He has gone there, and He has lighted up with the glory of immortality those dark abodes of the dead. Our brother, whom we now commit to the grave, we do not bid farewell to for ever. We shall see him once again; for it is said: "Blessed are the dead who die in the Lord; they rest from their labours, and their works do follow them." He has a work to do even there—he has something to do for God where he has gone. But let us, who hope to share in his prayers at the throne of mercy, help him now in our prayers, for we know not, in the judgment of God, what faults and imperfections there may be even in that pure, guileless soul. Eternal rest give to him, O Lord, and let perpetual light shine upon him. May his soul and the souls of all the faithful departed, through the mercy of God, rest in peace. Amen.

The absolutions were then given, the funeral procession formed, and Canon Brownlow performed the last rites at the Mortlake cemetery.

Farewell, dear and loving friend, until we meet in eternity! May thy example stir up our slothful apathetic hearts to imitate thy zeal in the service of God! May this record of thy life and labours stimulate some to carry out that work for the African Missions that lay so near to thy faithful heart! And may the memory of thy virtues console those whom thou hast left behind in this vale of tears!

> Farewell, but not for ever, brother dear!
> Angels, to whom the willing task is given,
> Shall tend, and nurse, and lull thee, as thou liest;
> And Masses on the earth, and prayers in Heaven,
> Shall aid thee at the throne of the Most Highest!

Requiescat in pace.

SELECTION

FROM

BURNS & OATES'

Catalogue

OF

PUBLICATIONS.

LONDON: BURNS AND OATES, Lᴅ.

ORCHARD ST., W., & 63 PATERNOSTER ROW, E.C.

NEW YORK: 9 BARCLAY STREET.

1890.

NEW BOOKS.

Natural Religion. Being Vol. I. of Dr. HETTINGER'S "Evidences of Christianity." Edited, with an introduction on CERTAINTY, by the Rev. H. S. Bowden, of the Oratory, with the Author's approval. Crown 8vo, cloth, 7s. 6d.

Letters of St. Augustine. Selected and arranged by MARY H. ALLIES. New volume. Quarterly Series (No. 73). Cloth, 6s. 6d.

The Church of my Baptism, and why I returned to it. By FRANCIS KING. Crown 8vo, cloth, 2s. 6d.

Life of St. Justin (Martyr.) By Mrs. CHARLES MARTIN (Author of "Life of St. Jerome"). Cloth, gilt, 2s.

The One Mediator; or, Sacrifice and Sacraments. By WILLIAM HUMPHREY, Priest of the Society of Jesus. Crown 8vo, cloth, 5s.

The Life of Don Bosco, Founder of the Salesian Society. Translated from the French of J. M. Villefranche, by LADY MARTIN. With a Portrait of Don Bosco. Second Edition. Crown 8vo. Cloth, 4s. 6d.

History of the sufferings of Eighteen Carthusians in England, who, refusing to take part in Schism, and to separate themselves from the Unity of the Catholic Church were cruelly martyred. Translated from the Latin of DOM MAURICE CHAUNCY, a professed Member of the London Charter House. Quarto, cloth, 3s.

Our Lady's Dowry. How England won that title. By the Rev. T. E. BRIDGETT, C.SS.R. New and enlarged edition. Crown 8vo, cloth, 5s.

The Perfection of Man by Charity: A Spiritual Treatise. By the Rev. FATHER REGINALD BUCKLER, O.P. Crown 8vo, cloth, 5s.

The Life of St. Patrick, Apostle of Ireland. By the Rev. W. B. MORRIS, of the Oratory. Fourth Edition. Crown 8vo, cloth, 5s.

Plain Sermons. By the Rev. R. D. BROWNE. Sixty-four Plain Sermons on the fundamental truths of the Catholic Church. Crown 8vo, cloth, 6s.

The Pilgrim's Handbook to Jerusalem and its neighbourhood. By WILFRID C. ROBINSON. From the French of Frère Liévin de Hamme, O.S.F., Resident at Jerusalem. With Map and Plans. Fcap. 8vo, cloth, 3s. 6d.

My Time, and what I've done with it. An Autobiography. Compiled from the Diary, Notes, and Personal Recollections of Cecil Colvin, Son of Sir John Colvin, Bart., of the late Firm of Colvin, Cavander & Co. By F. C. BURNAND. With Portrait of the Author. Crown 8vo, cloth, 5s.

SELECTION

BURNS AND OATES' CATALOGUE
OF PUBLICATIONS.

—➤➤➤✦✦◄◄◄—

ALLIES, T. W. (K.C.S.G.)

Formation of Christendom. Vols. I., II., III. . each	£0	12	0
Church and State as seen in the Formation of Christendom, 8vo, pp. 472, cloth	0	14	0
The Throne of the Fisherman, built by the Carpenter's Son, the Root, the Bond, and the Crown of Christendom. Demy 8vo . . . . . ;	0	10	0
The Holy See and the Wandering of the Nations. Demy 8vo.	0	10	6

"It would be quite superfluous at this hour of the day to recommend Mr. Allies' writings to English Catholics. Those of our readers who remember the article on his writings in the *Katholik*, know that he is esteemed in Germany as one of our foremost writers."—*Dublin Review.*

ALLIES, MARY.

Leaves from St. John Chrysostom, With introduction by T. W. Allies, K.C.S.G. Crown 8vo, cloth .	0	6	0

"Miss Allies 'Leaves' are delightful reading; the English is remarkably pure and graceful; page after page reads as if it were original. No commentator, Catholic or Protestant, has ever surpassed St. John Chrysostom in the knowledge of Holy Scripture, and his learning was of a kind which is of service now as it was at the time when the inhabitants of a great city hung on his words."—*Tablet.*

ALLNATT, C. F. B.

Cathedra Petri. Third and Enlarged Edition. Paper.	0	5	0

"Invaluable to the controversialist and the theologian, and most useful for educated men inquiring after truth or anxious to know the positive testimony of Christian antiquity in favour of Papal claims."—*Month.*

Which is the True Church? New Edition . .	0	1	4
The Church and the Sects.	0	1	0
Ditto, Ditto. Second Series. . . .	0	1	6

ANNUS SANCTUS:

Hymns of the Church for the Ecclesiastical Year. Translated from the Sacred Offices by various Authors, with Modern, Original, and other Hymns, and an Appendix of Earlier Versions. Selected and Arranged by ORBY SHIPLEY, M.A.

Popular edition, in two parts . . each	0	1	0
In stiff boards	0	3	6
Plain Cloth, lettered	0	5	0
Edition de luxe	0	10	6

ANSWERS TO ATHEISTS: OR NOTES ON

Ingersoll. By the Rev. A. Lambert, (over 100,000 copies sold in America). Ninth edition. Paper. £0 0 6

Cloth 0 1 0

B. N.

The Jesuits: their Foundation and History. 2 vols. crown 8vo, cloth, red edges 0 15 0

"The book is just what it professes to be—*a popular history*, drawn from well-known sources," &c.—*Month*.

BACQUEZ, L'ABBE.

The "Divine Office": From the French of l'Abbé Bacquez, of the Seminary of St. Sulpice, Paris. Edited by the Rev. Father Taunton, of the Congregation of the Oblates of St. Charles. Cloth . . . 0 6 0

"The translation of this most edifying work from the walls of St. Sulpice, the source of so much sacerdotal perfection, comes to us most opportunely, and we heartily commend it to the use of the clergy and of the faithful." THE CARDINAL ARCHBISHOP OF WESTMINSTER.
"A very complete manual, learned, wholesome, and devout."—*Saturday Review*.

BORROMEO, LIFE OF ST. CHARLES.

From the Italian of Peter Guissano. 2 vols. . . 0 15 0

"A standard work, which has stood the test of succeeding ages; it is certainly the finest work on St. Charles in an English dress."—*Tablet*.

BOWDEN, REV. H. S. (of the Oratory) Edited by.

Dante's Divina Commedia: Its scope and value. From the German of FRANCIS HETTINGER, D.D. With an engraving of Dante. Crown 8vo . . 0 10 6

"All that Venturi attempted to do has been now approached with far greater power and learning by Dr. Hettinger, who, as the author of the 'Apologie des Christenthums,' and as a great Catholic theologian, is eminently well qualified for the task he has undertaken."—*The Saturday Review*.

BRIDGETT, REV. T. E. (C.SS.R.).

Discipline of Drink 0 3 6

"The historical information with which the book abounds gives evidence of deep research and patient study, and imparts a permanent interest to the volume, which will elevate it to a position of authority and importance enjoyed by few of its compeers."—*The Arrow*.

Our Lady's Dowry; how England Won and Lost that Title. New and Enlarged Edition. . . . 0 5 0

"This book is the ablest vindication of Catholic devotion to Our Lady, drawn from tradition, that we know of in the English language."—*Tablet*.

Ritual of the New Testament. An essay on the principles and origin of Catholic Ritual in reference to the New Testament. Third edition 0 5 0

BRIDGETT, REV. T. E. (C.SS.R.)—*continued*.

The Life of the Blessed John Fisher. With a reproduction of the famous portrait of Blessed JOHN FISHER by HOLBEIN, and other Illustrations. Cloth £0 7 6
"The Life of Blessed John Fisher could hardly fail to be interesting and instructive. Sketched by Father Bridgett's practised pen, the portrait of this holy martyr is no less vividly displayed in the printed pages of the book than in the wonderful picture of Holbein, which forms the frontispiece."—*Tablet.*

The True Story of the Catholic Hierarchy deposed by Queen Elizabeth, with fuller Memoirs of its Last Two Survivors. By the Rev. T. E. BRIDGETT, C.SS.R., and the late Rev. T. F. KNOX, D.D., of the London Oratory. Crown 8vo, cloth, 0 7 6
" We have to express our obligation to Father Bridgett for the volume he has given us. It is full of instruction and interest, will correct many popular impressions, and manifests on every page an industry and exactness which in these days is rare."—*Dublin Review.*
" We gladly acknowledge the value of this work on a subject which has been obscured by prejudice and carelessness."—*Saturday Review.*

BRIDGETT, REV. T. E. (C.SS.R.), Edited by.

Souls Departed. By CARDINAL ALLEN. First published in 1565, now edited in modern spelling by the Rev. T. E. Bridgett 0 6 0

CASWALL, FATHER.

Catholic Latin Instructor in the Principal Church Offices and Devotions, for the Use of Choirs, Convents, and Mission Schools, and for Self-Teaching. 1 vol., complete 0 3 6
Or Part I., containing Benediction, Mass, Serving at Mass, and various Latin Prayers in ordinary use . 0 1 6
May Pageant : A Tale of Tintern. (A Poem) Second edition 0 2 0
Poems 0 5 0
Lyra Catholica, containing all the Breviary and Missal Hymns, with others from various sources. 32mo, cloth, red edges 0 2 6

CATHOLIC BELIEF: OR, A SHORT AND

Simple Exposition of Catholic Doctrine. By the Very Rev. Joseph Faà di Bruno, D.D. Ninth edition . . . . . Price 6d.; post free, 0 0 8½
Cloth, lettered, ... 0 0 10
Also an edition on better paper and bound in cloth, with gilt lettering and steel frontispiece 0 2 0

CHALLONER, BISHOP.

Meditations for every day in the year. New edition. Revised and edited by the Right Rev. John Virtue, D.D., Bishop of Portsmouth. 8vo. 5th edition . 0 3 0
And in other bindings.

COLERIDGE, REV. H. J. (S.J.)
(See Quarterly Series.)

DEHARBE, FATHER JOSEPH, (S.J.)

A History of Religion, or the Evidences of the Divinity of the Christian Religion, as furnished by its History from the Creation of the World to our own Times. Designed as a Help to Catechetical Instruction in Schools and Churches. Pp. 628. . . . . net £0 8 6

DEVAS, C. S.

Studies of Family Life: a contribution to Social Science. Crown 8vo 0 5 0
"We recommend these pages and the remarkable evidence brought together in them to the careful attention of all who are interested in the well-being of our common humanity."—*Guardian.*
"Both thoughtful and stimulating."—*Saturday Review.*

DRANE, AUGUSTA THEODOSIA

History of St. Catherine of Siena and her Companions. A new edition in two vols. 0 12 6
"It has been reserved for the author of the present work to give us complete biography of St. Catherine. . . . Perhaps the greatest success of the writer is the way in which she has contrived to make the Saint herself live in the pages of the book."—*Tablet.*

EYRE, MOST REV. CHARLES, (Abp. of Glasgow).

The History of St. Cuthbert: or, An Account of his Life, Decease, and Miracles. Third edition. Illustrated with maps, charts, &c., and handsomely bound in cloth. Royal 8vo 0 14 0
"A handsome, well appointed volume, in every way worthy of its illustrious subject. . . . The chief impression of the whole is the picture of a great and good man drawn by a sympathetic hand."—*Spectator.*

FABER, REV. FREDERICK WILLIAM, (D.D.)

All for Jesus	0 5 0
Bethlehem	0 7 0
Blessed Sacrament	0 7 6
Creator and Creature	0 6 0
Ethel's Book of the Angels.	0 5 0
Foot of the Cross	0 6 0
Growth in Holiness	0 6 0
Hymns	0 6 0
Notes on Doctrinal and Spiritual Subjects, 2 vols. each	0 5 0
Poems	0 5 0
Precious Blood	0 5 0
Sir Lancelot	0 5 0
Spiritual Conferences	0 6 0
Life and Letters of Frederick William Faber, D.D., Priest of the Oratory of St. Philip Neri. By John Edward Bowden of the same Congregation . .	0 6 0

FOLEY, REV. HENRY, (S.J.)

Records of the English Province of the Society of
Jesus. Vol. I., Series I. . . . . net £1 6 0
Vol. II., Series II., III., IV. . . . net 1 6 0
Vol. III., Series V., VI., VII., VIII. . . net 1 10 0
Vol. IV. Series IX., X., XI. . . . . net 1 6 0
Vol. V., Series XII. with nine Photographs of
Martyrs . . . . net 1 10 0
Vol. VI., Diary and Pilgrim-Book of the English Col-
lege, Rome. The Diary from 1579 to 1773, with
Biographical and Historical Notes. The Pilgrim-
Book of the Ancient English Hospice attached to
the College from 1580 to 1656, with Historical
Notes . . . . net 1 6 0
Vol. VII. Part the First : General Statistics of the Pro-
vince ; and Collectanea, giving Biographical Notices
of its Members and of many Irish and Scotch Jesuits.
With 20 Photographs . . . . . net 1 6 0
Vol. VII. Part the Second : Collectanea, Completed ;
With Appendices. Catalogues of Assumed and Real
Names : Annual Letters ; Biographies and Miscel-
lanea. . . . . net 1 6 0

"As a biographical dictionary of English Jesuits, it deserves a
place in every well-selected library, and, as a collection of marvellous occurrences, persecutions, martyrdoms, and evidences of the
results of faith, amongst the books of all who belong to the Catholic
Church."—*Genealogist.*

FORMBY, REV. HENRY.

Monotheism : in the main derived from the Hebrew
nation and the Law of Moses. The Primitive Religion of the City of Rome. An historical Investiga-
tion. Demy 8vo. 0 5 0

FRANCIS DE SALES, ST. : THE WORKS OF.

Translated into the English Language by the Rev.
H. B. Mackey, O.S.B., under the direction of the
Right Rev. Bishop Hedley, O.S.B. . . .
Vol. I. Letters to Persons in the World. Cloth . 0 6 0

"The letters must be read in order to comprehend the charm and
sweetness of their style."—*Tablet.*

Vol. II.—The Treatise on the Love of God. Father
Carr's translation of 1630 has been taken as a basis,
but it has been modernized and thoroughly revised
and corrected. 0 9 0

"To those who are seeking perfection by the path of contemplation
this volume will be an armoury of help."—*Saturday Review.*

Vol. III. The Catholic Controversy. . . 0 6 0

"No one who has not read it can conceive how clear, how convinc-
ing, and how well adapted to our present needs are these controversial
'leaves.'"—*Tablet.*

FRANCIS DE SALES, ST.: WORKS OF.—*continued.*

Vol. IV. Letters to Persons in Religion, with introduction by Bishop Hedley on "St. Francis de Sales and the Religious State." £0   6   0

"The sincere piety and goodness, the grave wisdom, the knowledge of human nature, the tenderness for its weakness, and the desire for its perfection that pervade the letters, make them pregnant of instruction for all serious persons. The translation and editing have been admirably done."—*Scotsman.*

    ⁎⁎ Other vols. in preparation.

GALLWEY, REV. PETER, (S.J.)

Precious Pearl of Hope in the Mercy of God, The. Translated from the Italian. With Preface by the Rev. Father Gallwey. Cloth   0   4   6

Lectures on Ritualism and on the Anglican Orders. 2 vols. (Or may be had separately.)   0   8   0

Salvage from the Wreck. A few Memories of the Dead, preserved in Funeral Discourses. With Portraits. Crown 8vo.   0   7   6

GIBSON, REV. H.

Catechism Made Easy. Being an Explanation of the Christian Doctrine. Fourth edition. 2 vols., cloth   0   7   6

"This work must be of priceless worth to any who are engaged in any form of catechetical instruction. It is the best book of the kind that we have seen in English."—*Irish Monthly.*

GILLOW, JOSEPH.

Literary and Biographical History, or, Bibliographical Dictionary of the English Catholics. From the Breach with Rome, in 1534, to the Present Time. Vols. *I., II. and III. cloth, demy 8vo* .   . *each.*   0   15   0

    ⁎⁎ Other vols. in preparation.

"The patient research of Mr. Gillow, his conscientious record of minute particulars, and especially his exhaustive bibliographical information in connection with each name, are beyond praise."—*British Quarterly Review.*

The Haydock Papers. Illustrated. Demy 8vo.   .   0   7   6

" We commend this collection to the attention of every one that is interested in the records of the sufferings and struggles of our ancestors to hand down the faith to their children. It is in the perusal of such details that we bring home to ourselves the truly heroic sacrifices that our forefathers endured in those dark and dismal times."—*Tablet.*

GROWTH IN THE KNOWLEDGE OF OUR LORD.

Meditations for every Day in the Year, exclusive of those for Festivals, Days of Retreat, &c. Adapted from the original of Abbé de Brandt, by Sister Mary Fidelis. A new and Improved Edition, in 3 Vols. Sold only in sets. Price per set,   .   .   .   1   2   6

" The praise, though high, bestowed on these excellent meditations by the Bishop of Salford is well deserved. The language, like good spectacles, spreads treasures before our vision without attracting attention to itself."—*Dublin Review.*

HEDLEY, BISHOP.

Our Divine Saviour, and other Discourses. Crown 8vo. £0 6 0

"A distinct and noteworthy feature of these sermons is, we certainly think, their freshness—freshness of thought, treatment, and style ; nowhere do we meet pulpit commonplace or hackneyed phrase —everywhere, on the contrary, it is the heart of the preacher pouring out to his flock his own deep convictions, enforcing them from the 'Treasures, old and new,' of a cultivated mind."—*Dublin Review.*

HUMPHREY, REV. W. (S.J.)

Suarez on the Religious State : A Digest of the Doctrine contained in his Treatise, "De Statû Religionis." 3 vols., pp. 1200. Cloth, roy. 8vo. . . . 1 10 0

"This laborious and skilfully executed work is a distinct addition to English theological literature. Father Humphrey's style is quiet, methodical, precise, and as clear as the subject admits. Every one will be struck with the air of legal exposition which pervades the book. He takes a grip of his author, under which the text yields up every atom of its meaning and force."—*Dublin Review.*

LEDOUX, REV. S. M.

History of the Seven Holy Founders of the Order of the Servants of Mary. Crown 8vo, cloth . . 0 4 6

"Throws a full light upon the Seven Saints recently canonized, whom we see as they really were. All that was marvellous in their call, their works, and their death is given with the charm of a picturesque and speaking style."—*Messenger of the Sacred Heart.*

LEE, REV. F. G., D.D. (of All Saints, Lambeth.)

Edward the Sixth : Supreme Head. Second edition. Crown 8vo 0 6 0

"In vivid interest and in literary power, no less than in solid historical value, Dr. Lee's present work comes fully up to the standard of its predecessors ; and to say that is to bestow high praise. The book evinces Dr. Lee's customary diligence of research in amassing facts, and his rare artistic power in welding them into a harmonious and effective whole."—*John Bull.*

LIFE OF FATHER CHAMPAGNAT

Founder of the Society of the Little Brothers of Mary. Containing a portrait of Fr. CHAMPAGNAT, and four full page illustrations. Demy 8vo 0 8 0

"A serious and able essay on the science and art of the Christian education of children, exemplified in the career of one who gave his life to it."—*Dublin Review.*

LIGUORI, ST. ALPHONSUS.

New and Improved Translation of the Complete Works of St. Alphonsus, edited by the late Bishop Coffin :—
Vol. 1. The Christian Virtues, and the Means for Obtaining them. Cloth elegant 0 4 0
Or separately :—
1. The Love of our Lord Jesus Christ . . . 0 1 4
2. Treatise on Prayer. *(In the ordinary editions a great part of this work is omitted)* . . . 0 1 4
3. A Christian's rule of Life 0 1 0

LIGUORI, ST. ALPHONSUS.—*continued*.

Vol. II, The Mysteries of the Faith—The Incarnation ;
containing Meditations and Devotions on the Birth
and Infancy of Jesus Christ, &c., suited for Advent
and Christmas. £0 3 6
   Cheap edition 0 2 0
Vol. III. The Mysteries of the Faith—The Blessed
Sacrament 0 3 6
   Cheap edition 0 2 0
Vol. IV. Eternal Truths—Preparation for Death . 0 3 6
   Cheap edition 0 2 0
Vol. V. Treatises on the Passion, containing "Jesus
hath loved us," &c. 0 3 0
   Cheap edition 0 2 0
Vol. VI. Glories of Mary. New edition . . . 0 3 6
   With Frontispiece, cloth 0 4 6
   Also in better bindings.

LIVIUS, REV. T. (M.A., C.SS.R.)

St. Peter, Bishop of Rome ; or, the Roman Episcopate
of the Prince of the Apostles, proved from the
Fathers, History and Chronology, and illustrated by
arguments from other sources. Dedicated to his
Eminence Cardinal Newman. Demy 8vo, cloth . 0 12 0
Explanation of the Psalms and Canticles in the Divine
Office. By ST. ALPHONSUS LIGUORI. Translated
from the Italian by THOMAS LIVIUS, C.SS.R.
With a Preface by his Eminence Cardinal MANNING.
Crown 8vo, cloth 0 7 6

MANNING, CARDINAL.

Blessed Sacrament the Centre of Immutable Truth.
   Second edition 0 1 0
Confidence in God. Fourth edition 0 1 0
England and Christendom 0 10 6
Eternal Priesthood. Eighth Edition 0 2 6
Four Great Evils of the Day. Fifth Edition. Paper 0 2 6
   Cloth 0 3 6
Fourfold Sovereignty of God. Third edition Paper 0 2 6
   Cloth 0 3 6
Glories of the Sacred Heart. Fifth edition. . . 0 6 0
Grounds of Faith. Eighth edition. 0 1 6
Holy Gospel of our Lord Jesus Christ according to St.
   John. With a Preface by His Eminence. . . 0 1 0
Religio Viatoris. Third Edition. Wrapper. . . 0 1 0
   Cloth. 0 2 0
Independence of the Holy See. Second Edition. . 0 5 0
Internal Mission of the Holy Ghost. Fourth edition . 0 8 6
Love of Jesus to Penitents. Eighth edition . . 0 1 6
Miscellanies. 3 vols. . . . . . each 0 6 0

MANNING, CARDINAL—*continued.*

Office of the Holy Ghost under the Gospel . . . £0	1	0
Petri Privilegium 0	10	6
Praise, A Sermon on ; with an Indulgenced Devotion. 0	1	0
Sermons on Ecclesiastical Subjects. Vols. I. II. and		
III. . . . . each 0	6	0
Sin and its Consequences. Seventh edition. . . 0	6	0
Temporal Mission of the Holy Ghost. Third edition . 0	8	6
Temporal Power of the Pope. Third edition . . 0	5	0
The Office of the Church in Higher Education . . 0	0	6
True Story of the Vatican Council. Second Edition . 0	5	0
National Education 0	2	6

MANNING, CARDINAL, Edited by.

Life of the Curé of Ars. New edition, enlarged. . 0 4 0

MIVART, PROF. ST. GEORGE (M.D., F.R.S.)

Nature and Thought. Second edition . . . 0 4 0

"The complete command of the subject, the wide grasp, the subtlety, the readiness of illustration, the grace of style, contrive to render this one of the most admirable books of its class."—*British Quarterly Review.*

A Philosophical Catechism. Fifth edition . 0 1 0

"It should become the *vade mecum* of Catholic students."—*Tablet.*

MONTGOMERY, HON. MRS.

Approved by the Most Rev. George Porter, Archbishop of Bombay.

The Divine Sequence : A Treatise on Creation and
Redemption. Cloth 0 3 6

The Eternal Years. With an Introduction by the
Most Rev. George Porter, Archbishop of Bombay.
Cloth 0 3 6

The Divine Ideal. Cloth 0 3 6

" A work of original thought carefully developed and expressed in lucid and richly imaged style."—*Tablet.*

" The writing of a pious, thoughtful, earnest woman."—*Church Review.*

" Full of truth, and sound reason, and confidence."—*American Catholic Book News.*

MORRIS, REV. JOHN (S.J.)

Letter Books of Sir Amias Poulet, keeper of Mary
Queen of Scots. Demy 8vo 0 10 6

Troubles of our Catholic Forefathers, related by themselves. Second Series. 8vo, cloth. . . . 0 14 0

Third Series 0 14 0

The Life of Father John Gerard, S.J. Third edition,
rewritten and enlarged 0 14 0

The Life and Martyrdom of St. Thomas Becket. Second
and enlarged edition. In one volume, large post 8vo,
cloth, pp. xxxvi., 632, ... 0 12 6

or bound in two parts, cloth 0 13 0

MURPHY, J. N.

    Chair of Peter.   Third edition, with the statistics, &c.,
    brought down to the present day.   720 pages.
    Crown 8vo . . . .   *£*0 6 0

    "In a series of clearly written chapters, precise in statement,
excellently temperate in tone, the author deals with just those
questions regarding the power, claims; and history of the
Roman Pontiff which are at the present time of most actual interest."
—Dublin Review.

NEWMAN, CARDINAL.

Annotated Translation of Athanasius. 2 vols. . each	0	7	6
Apologia pro Vitâ suâ	0	6	0
Arians of the Fourth Century, The	0	6	0
Callista. An Historical Tale.	0	6	0
Church of the Fathers	0	4	0
Difficulties of Anglicans. Two volumes—			
Vol. I. Twelve Lectures	0	7	6
Vol. II. Letter to Dr. Pusey and to the Duke of			
Norfolk	0	5	6
Discussions and Arguments	0	6	0
Doctrine of Justification	0	5	0
Dream of Gerontius	0	0	6
Essay on Assent	0	7	6
Essay on the Development of Christian Doctrine .	0	6	0
Essays Critical and Historical. Two volumes, with			
Notes . . . . each	0	6	0
Essays on Miracles, Two. 1. Of Scripture. 2. Of			
Ecclesiastical History	0	6	0
Historical Sketches. Three volumes . . . each	0	6	0
Idea of a University. Lectures and Essays . .	0	7	0
Loss and Gain. Ninth Edition	0	5	6
Occasional Sermons	0	6	0
Parochial and Plain Sermons. Eight volumes. . each	0	5	0
Present Position of Catholics in England. . .	0	7	0
Sermons on Subjects of the Day.	0	5	0
Sermons to Mixed Congregations	0	6	0
Theological Tracts	0	8	0
University Sermons	0	5	0
Verses on Various Occasions.	0	6	0
Via Media. Two volumes, with Notes . . each	0	6	0

NORTHCOTE, VERY REV. J. S. (D.D.)

    Roma Sotterranea; or, An Account of the Roman
Catacombs.   New edition.   Re-written and greatly
enlarged.   This work is in three volumes, which
may at present be had separately—

Vol. I. History	1	4	0
Vol. II. Christian Art.	1	4	0
Vol. III. Epitaphs of the Catacombs . .	0	10	0
The Second and Third Volumes may also be had			
bound together in cloth	1	12	0

NORTHCOTE, VERY REV. J. S. (D.D.)—*continued.*

Visit to the Roman Catacombs: Being a popular
abridgment of the larger work. £0 4 0
Mary in the Gospels 0 3 6

PAYNE, JOHN ORLEBAR, (M.A.)

Records of the English Catholics of 1715. Demy 8vo.
Half-bound, gilt top 0 15 0

"A book of the kind Mr. Payne has given us would have astonish-
ed Bishop Milner or Dr. Lingard. They would have treasured it,
for both of them knew the value of minute fragments of historical
information. The Editor has derived nearly the whole of the information which he has given, from unprinted sources, and we must
congratulate him on having found a few incidents here and there
which may bring the old times back before us in a most touching
manner."—*Tablet.*

English Catholic Non-Jurors of 1715. Being a Sum-
mary of the Register of their Estates, with Genea-
logical and other Notes, and an Appendix of
Unpublished Documents in the Public Record
Office. In one Volume. Demy 8vo. . . . 1 1 0

"Most carefully and creditably brought out . . . From first to last,
full of social interest and biographical details, for which we may
search in vain elsewhere."—*Antiquarian Magazine.*

Old English Catholic Missions. Demy 8vo, half-bound. 0 7 6

" A book to hunt about in for curious odds and ends."—*Saturday
Review.*

"These registers tell us in their too brief records, teeming with interest for all their scantiness, many a tale of patient heroism."—*Tablet.*

POOR SISTERS OF NAZARETH, THE.

A descriptive Sketch of Convent Life. By Alice Meynell.
Profusely Illustrated with Drawings especially made
by George Lambert. Large 4to. Boards . . 0 2 6
A limited number of copies are also issued as an *Edition
de Luxe,* containing proofs of the illustrations printed
on one side only of the paper, and handsomely bound. 0 10 6

"Bound in a most artistic cover, illustrated with a naturalness
that could only have been born of powerful sympathy; printed clearly,
neatly, and on excellent paper, and written with the point, aptness,
and ripeness of style which we have learnt to associate with Mrs.
Meynell's literature."—*Tablet.*

"Mrs. Meynell has seldom written anything more simply and
tenderly beautiful. She writes not only brightly and charmingly,
but very humanly as well."—*Manchester Examiner.*

" A beautifully got-up volume, which will make Nazareth House
even better known than it already is, and for that reason, as well as
for its merits, deserve success."—*Athenæum.*

POPE, THOMAS ALDER, M.A. (of the Oratory.)

Life of St. Philip Neri, Apostle of Rome. From the
Italian of Alfonso Capecelatro. 2 vols . . . 0 15 0

"No former life has given us so full a knowledge of the surroundings of St. Philip. . . . To those who have not read the original we
can say, with the greatest confidence, that they will find in these
two well-edited volumes a very large store of holy reading and of interesting history."—*Dublin Review.*

QUARTERLY SERIES Edited by the Rev. H. J.
Coleridge, S.J. 73 volumes published to date.

Selection.

The Life and Letters of St. Francis Xavier. By the Rev. H. J. Coleridge, S.J. 2 vols.	£0	10	6
The History of the Sacred Passion. By Father Luis de la Palma, of the Society of Jesus. Translated from the Spanish.	0	5	0
The Life of Dona Louisa de Carvajal. By Lady Georgiana Fullerton. Small edition	0	3	6
The Life and Letters of St. Teresa. 3 vols. By Rev. H. J. Coleridge, S.J. . . . . each	0	7	6
The Life of Mary Ward. By Mary Catherine Elizabeth Chalmers, of the Institute of the Blessed Virgin. Edited by the Rev. H. J. Coleridge, S.J. 2 vols.	0	15	0
The Return of the King. Discourses on the Latter Days. By the Rev. H. J. Coleridge, S.J. .	0	7	6
Pious Affections towards God and the Saints. Meditations for every Day in the Year, and for the Principal Festivals. From the Latin of the Ven. Nicolas Lancicius, S.J.	0	7	6
The Life and Teaching of Jesus Christ in Meditations for Every Day in the Year. By Fr. Nicolas Avancino, S.J. Two vols.	0	10	6
The Baptism of the King : Considerations on the Sacred Passion. By the Rev. H. J. Coleridge, S.J. .	0	7	6
The Mother of the King. Mary during the Life of Our Lord.	0	7	6
The Hours of the Passion. Taken from the *Life of Christ* by Ludolph the Saxon	0	7	6
The Mother of the Church. Mary during the first Apostolic Age	0	6	0
The Life of St. Bridget of Sweden. By the late F. J. M. A. Partridge	0	6	0
The Teachings and Counsels of St. Francis Xavier. From his Letters	0	5	0
Garcia Moreno, President of Ecuador. 1821—1875. From the French of the Rev. P. A. Berthe, C.SS.R. By Lady Herbert	0	7	6
The Life of St. Alonso Rodriguez. By Francis Goldie, of the Society of Jesus	0	7	6
Letters of St. Augustine. Selected and arranged by Mary H. Allies	0	6	6

VOLUMES ON THE LIFE OF OUR LORD.
The Holy Infancy.

The Preparation of the Incarnation .	0	7	6
The Nine Months. The Life of our Lord in the Womb.	0	7	6
The Thirty Years. Our Lord's Infancy and Early Life.	0	7	6

The Public Life of Our Lord.

The Ministry of St. John Baptist .	0	6	6

QUARTERLY SERIES—*(selection) continued.*

	£	s	d
The Preaching of the Beatitudes	£0	6	6
The Sermon on the Mount. Continued. 2 Parts, each	0	6	6
The Training of the Apostles. Parts I., II., III., IV. each	0	6	6
The Preaching of the Cross. Part I. . . .	0	6	6
The Preaching of the Cross. Parts II., III. each	0	6	0
Passiontide. Parts I. and II., each . . .	0	6	6
Chapters on the Parables of Our Lord . . .	0	7	6

Introductory Volumes.

The Life of our Life. Harmony of the Life of Our Lord, with Introductory Chapters and Indices. Two vols. (Reprinting.)

The Works and Words of our Saviour, gathered from the Four Gospels	0	7	6
The Story of the Gospels. Harmonised for Meditation	0	7	6

Full lists on application.

RAM, MRS. ABEL.

"Emmanuel." Being the Life of Our Lord Jesus Christ reproduced in the Mysteries of the Tabernacle. By Mrs. Abel Ram, author of "The most Beautiful among the Children of Men," &c. Crown 8vo, cloth — 0 5 0

" The foundation of the structure is laid with the greatest skill and the deepest knowledge of what constitutes true religion, and every chapter ends with an eloquent and soul-inspiring appeal for one or other of the virtues which the different scenes in the life of Our Saviour set prominently into view."—*Catholic Times.*

RAWES, THE LATE REV. Fr., Edited by.

The Library of the Holy Ghost :—
Vol. I. St. Thomas Aquinas on the Adorable Sacrament of the Altar. With Prayers and Thanksgivings for Holy Communion. Red cloth . . . 0 5 0
Little Books of the Holy Ghost:—(List on application.)

RICHARDS, REV. WALTER J. B. (D.D.)

Manual of Scripture History. Being an Analysis of the Historical Books of the Old Testament. By the Rev. W. J. B. Richards, D.D., Oblate of St. Charles ; Inspector of Schools in the Diocese of Westminster. Cloth 0 4 0

"Happy indeed will those children and young persons be who acquire in their early days the inestimably precious knowledge which these books impart."—*Tablet.*

RYDER, REV. H. I. D. (of the Oratory.)

Catholic Controversy: A Reply to Dr. Littledale's "Plain Reasons." Sixth edition 0 2 6

" Father Ryder of the Birmingham Oratory, has now furnished in a small volume a masterly reply to this assailant from without. The lighter charms of a brilliant and graceful style are added to the solid merits of this handbook of contemporary controversy."—*Irish Monthly.*

SOULIER, REV. P.
Life of St. Philip Benizi, of the Order of the Servants
of Mary.   Crown 8vo £0   8   0
"A clear and interesting account of the life and labours of this
eminent Servant of Mary."—*American Catholic Quarterly.*
"Very scholar-like, devout and complete."—*Dublin Review.*

STANTON, REV. R. (of the Oratory.)
A Menology of England and Wales ; or, Brief Mem-
orials of the British and English Saints, arranged
according to the Calendar.   Together with the Martyrs of the 16th and 17th centuries.   Compiled by
order of the Cardinal Archbishop and the Bishops
of the Province of Westminster.   Demy 8vo, cloth   0 14   0

THOMPSON, EDWARD HEALY, (M.A.)
The Life of Jean-Jacques Olier, Founder of the
Seminary of St. Sulpice.   New and Enlarged Edition.
Post 8vo, cloth, pp. xxxvi. 628   .   .   .   .   0 15   0
" It provides us with just what we most need, a model to look up to
and imitate ; one whose circumstances and surroundings were suffi-
ciently like our own to admit of an easy and direct application to our
own personal duties and daily occupations."—*Dublin Review.*
The Life and Glories of St. Joseph,   Husband of
Mary, Foster-Father of Jesus, and Patron of the
Universal Church.   Grounded on the Dissertations of
Canon Antonio Vitalis, Father José Moreno, and other
writers.   Crown 8vo, cloth, pp. xxvi., 488,   .   .   0   6   0

ULLATHORNE, ARCHBISHOP.
Endowments of Man, &c.   Popular edition.   .   .   0   7   0
Groundwork of the Christian Virtues : do.   .   .   0   7   0
Christian Patience,   .   .   do. do.   .   .   0   7   0
Ecclesiastical Discourses   0   6   0
Memoir of Bishop Willson.   0   2   6

WARD, WILFRID.
The Clothes of Religion. A reply to popular Positivism   0   3   6
"Very witty and interesting."—*Spectator.*
"Really models of what such essays should be."—*Church Quarterly
Review.*

WATERWORTH, REV. J.
The Canons and Decrees of the Sacred and Œcumenical
Council of Trent, celebrated under the Sovereign
Pontiffs, Paul III., Julius III., and Pius IV., tran-
slated by the Rev. J. WATERWORTH.   To which
are prefixed Essays on the External and Internal
History of the Council.   A new edition.   Demy
8vo, cloth 0 10   6

WISEMAN, CARDINAL.
Fabiola.   A Tale of the Catacombs. . . 3s. 6d. and   0   4   0
Also a new and splendid edition printed on large
quarto paper, embellished with thirty-one full-page
illustrations, and a coloured portrait of St. Agnes.
Handsomely bound.   1   1   0

www.ingramcontent.com/pod-product-compliance
Lightning Source LLC
Chambersburg PA
CBHW030540040726
47497CB00008B/2525

* 9 7 8 3 7 4 1 1 5 7 9 6 7 *